ALSO BY

DEREK THE GHOST

SCARY SCHOOL #1

SCARY SCHOOL #2
MONSTERS ON THE MARCH

SCARY SCHOOL #3
THE NORTHERN FRIGHTS

ZILLIONS OF ZOMBIES

BY

DEREK THE GHOST

ILLUSTRATIONS BY REVO YANSON

COVER ART BY MARCUS MULLER

Derek Taylor Kent Books

www.DerekTaylorKent.com

Library of Congress Cataloging-in-Publication Data
Kent, Derek Taylor.
    Zillions of Zombies / by Derek the Ghost ;
Illustrations by Revo Yanson — 1st ed.
        p. cm. — (Scary School ; #4)
    Summary: When a tussle at Monster Castle accidentally
flips a switch that turns all the zombies of the world to evil,
it's up to Charles Nukid and his friends to find the only
unicorn on Earth that can change them back to good before
the whole world is turned to zombies.
    ISBN ---------------------- (paperback bdg.)
        (1. Supernatural—Fiction.   2. Schools—Fiction.
        3. Zombies—Fiction.   4. Humorous Stories.) I.
        Yanson, Revo.,
        Ill. II. Title.

                    First Edition

TO ALL MY
SCARY SCHOOL FANS
WHO INSPIRED ME TO KEEP GOING!

CONTENTS

RE∙RE∙REINTRODUCTION
XII

ONE
ALL HAIL KING TOOTHPICK
1

TWO
THE DANCE OF DESTINY
8

THREE
RAMON THE ZOMBIE KID
18

FOUR
TURLOCK THE TINY TROLL
28

FIVE
ZOMBIE APOCALYPSE
37

SIX
THE PEP SQUAD
50

SEVEN
A GORGE OF GARBAGE
61

EIGHT
THE TEACHER WHO WASN'T THERE
66

NINE
A GIANT PROBLEM
79

TEN
MS MEDUSA
89

ELEVEN
CHUNKY THE EVIL DOLL
101

TWELVE
THE SWAMP OF CATASTROPHE
110

THIRTEEN
BRING YOUR PET TO SCHOOL DAY
117

FOURTEEN
NOT NICE SPRITES
123

FIFTEEN
DR JECKYLL AND MRS HYDE
128

SIXTEEN
THE BOG MONSTER
138

SEVENTEEN
PETUNIAS AND DODOS AND GIANTS —
OH MY!
144

EIGHTEEN
THE WORMASAUR
151

NINETEEN
THE THREE PATHS
157

TWENTY
THE VALLEY OF THE UNICORNS
163

TWENTY~ONE
THE DEATH OF KING TOOTHPICK
179

TWENTY~TWO
A FEW TOO MANY ZOMBIES
191

TWENTY~THREE
THE END OF SCARY SCHOOL
200

BONUS CHAPTER
222

CAVEAT
DISCIPULUS

RE∞RE∞
REINTRODUCTION

Welcome back, friends! It's me, the eleven-year-old ghost who has guided you safely through your time at Scary School. So far.

Do you remember my name? That's right! It's Derek the Ghost! How did you remember so quickly? Oh yeah, it's on the cover. Duh.

Sorry it took so long to get this book out to you, but after you read about what I and the students of Scary School have gone through, you'll be amazed I was able to survive, much less write a whole book about it. And before you ask, yes, ghosts can be double-killed. It's not easy. Only something truly terrifying can do it. And in this book, you will read all about it.

I know it's been a long time since our last adventure, so I should probably catch you up on everything that happened before. At the end of *Scary School #3: The Northern Frights*, Charles Nukid and his friends managed to miraculously defeat the enormous Ice Dragon and save all the monster students of Scream Academy.

When they returned, a parade thrown in their honor and the Dance of Destiny was announced. Charles was excited to go to the dance with his best friend, Penny Possum, but right after she said yes, a bearodactyl swooped down and carried him off to Monster Kingdom!

The bearodactyl told Charles that he had been declared the new monster king because he had defeated King Zog in battle (that happened in Book Two). He had no choice but to be the new ruler of all monsters.

Of course, that was the last thing Charles expected as a skinny kid without a hint of monster about him, but if you say no to a bearodactyl, that's probably the last thing you'll ever do. So, Charles smartly kept his mouth shut while the beast carried him across the ocean to Monster Kingdom.

You might also remember three boys asked Petunia to the Dance of Destiny— Johnny the sasquatch, Jason the hockey star, and Fred the boy without fear. To find out whom she went with, you'll have to read the Book Three "Bonus Chapter" at www.ScarySchool.com. After you do that you'll be all caught up.

All right, it's time to get started with our new story. But before you turn the page, a word of warning… if you're afraid of a very specific type of monster, you may not want to read any further because there are literally *zillions* of them in this book.

Care to guess which monster? That's right! It's Zombies! How did you—oh, that's right, you saw the cover. I keep forgetting that.

And so, as usual… good luck surviving your time at Scary School!

1

ALL HAIL KING TOOTHPICK

"Awoo-aloo, monsters, ghouls, mythical beasts, and all other ghastly creatures of Monster Kingdom. Thank you for stomping here today. It is my monstery honor to introduce the one who defeated King Zog in battle and is therefore our new monster king!"

Ms. Stingbottom's words rang out from atop Monster Castle to a crowd of monsters gathered on the hillside below. They seemed both excited and perplexed by what they were hearing. Was King Zog really going to willingly give up the throne? No monster had ever done that. Usually a fierce battle with a lot of clashing of tusks and thrashing of claws was involved.

After following the stinky trail of the bearodactyl that had carried Charles away, I arrived just in time to see Ms. Stingbottom, dressed in full queen regalia over her pink fur, lion's head, lobster claws, and scorpion tail, making the announcement.

The monsters in the crowd were climbing on top of one another to view the terrifying beast that had defeated King Zog. Little did they know it was an eleven-year-old boy with helmet hair who barely weighed more than the bones inside of him.

Because most monsters smell like words that shouldn't be in print, the whole hillside smelled like a garbage dump overflowing with old diapers and rotting fish.

When Queen Stingbottom stepped out on the balcony (I had no idea our monster math teacher from Book One was queen of the monsters) the crowd roared and howled. She continued, "When my husband, King Zog, and his army of karate monsters rose to power, we implemented the modern laws of monster manners and equality for all monsters, from the foul-smelling to the sweet-smelling. Among those laws it was decreed that a monster king or queen shall rule until they die or are defeated in battle. Well, it took some convincing on my part, but King Zog has agreed to give up the throne to the one who stood before an army of karate monsters and monster pirates and led his school to a resounding victory, all for the love of my daughter, Princess Zogette. Of course she then rejected him and decided to marry Captain Pigbeard instead, but that doesn't matter. Please give a monstrous greeting to your new monster king, who will no doubt install his own set of terrifying laws... Charles Nukid!"

Charles Nukid, the Scary School sixth-grader who was so skinny everyone called him "toothpick," was shoved out toward the ledge next to Queen Stingbottom. He was wearing a robe made of monster bones that was so long and heavy he had to hold onto the railing so not to fall backward.

All the roars and howls turned to instant quiet.

"That not a monster! That a human!" a furry monster shouted from the crowd.

"Are you sure?" said another monster. "It's so skinny it looks like a dragon's toothpick. Maybe it's a toothpick that learned to walk."

The crowd of monsters started chanting: "No King Toothpick! No King Toothpick!"

Charles sighed. Even in Monster Kingdom he couldn't escape that awful nickname.

Queen Stingbottom saw that things were not going well. She knew only one thing would calm down the monsters and prevent total chaos.

"Zog!" she bellowed through a curtain behind them. "Get out here and put your crown on this child!"

"No," said King Zog from inside. "I don't want to." Then his twenty-foot frog tongue shot out from inside and went "Pfffthth!" Queen Stingbottom snatched it between her huge lobster claws. "Get out here before I snap it off!"

"Okay, okay!"

King Zog rolled up his tongue and appeared from behind the curtain. All the monsters pointed and laughed. He covered his toad face with his walrus flippers. Charles picked up the scent of spring daisies in a morning field as he approached. There was a reason he was known as King Zog the Terrible, but Always Pleasant-Smelling.

"Har Har!" shouted an enormous filthy troll from the crowd. "How did you lose to that puny child?"

"Stop laughing at me! You didn't see his friends! They had coconuts!"

This made the monsters laugh even harder.

Charles noticed a tear rolling down King Zog's cheek.

"Let's just get this over with," Zog said. "A monster law is a monster law, so I must stick to it. Even though it's a dumb law."

He removed a crown made out of bearodactyl skulls and placed it over Charles's head. It was so large it slipped right down to his shoulders.

"There! Now he's new king," Zog declared with a whimper.

The crowd cheered, but Charles couldn't appreciate the moment because he felt bad for King Zog. Even though he attacked Scary School and put all of his friends in mortal danger, he was only doing what he thought was best for his daughter. While the idea of being the monster king would be a dream-come-true for any kid, especially for Charles, who loved monsters, he realized what he had to do.

"Quiet everyone!" Charles demanded.

The monster crowd hushed, scared of what the king's first decree would be. One time a monster king's first decree was for every monster to bring him the tentacle of a Kraken. That made for an eventful week.

"For my first order as monster king, I would like to renounce my crown and give it back to King Zog. Being your ruler would be super-cool, but I would rather go back to Scary School in time for the Dance of Destiny."

The crowd was aghast. Nobody had ever turned down the opportunity to be the monster king.

Queen Stingbottom leaned in. "I'm afraid you have no choice," she said. "Nobody will respect King Zog anymore. Besides, a monster law is the most important rule there is."

"A rule?" said Charles.

As I'm sure you remember, Charles loved following the rules. In fact, he hadn't broken one since he was three years old when he belched at the dinner table. He still hasn't forgiven himself for that one and gives himself a five-minute time-out every year on the anniversary in remembrance.

"Oh," said Charles. "Well, since I always follow the rules, I guess I have to be your monster king. Sorry, Zog."

"It okay," said Zog. "Me and Stingbottom already have a condo waiting for us in Monster Florida."

"What is your first decree?" a spiky-headed monster shouted to King Charles.

"Yes! Make us do something horrible to prove our loyalty!"

"Something horrible?" said Charles. "Hmmm. For my first decree, I order all monsters to um… go home and clean your caves!"

"Clean our caves?" said the spiky monster. "But, we haven't cleaned our caves in hundreds of years."

"You are so cruel!" a fluffy monster shouted.

"Show mercy!" begged a lizard-faced monster.

"That is the foulest decree of all time. Hail King Toothpick!" said a troll.

The crowd erupted, "Hail King Toothpick! Hail King Toothpick!"

Charles basked in their adoration and held up the crown.

"Well done," said Queen Stingbottom. "But now I have to show you your most important, most secret responsibility as the monster king. Follow me."

2

THE DANCE OF DESTINY

A few hours before Charles was being crowned monster king, he was taking part in the grand parade celebrating the successful exchange program with Scream Academy. As you may recall, it came to a dismal end when Charles accidentally stabbed the parade float with the Sword of Fire.

Afterward, the Dance of Destiny was announced, and Charles had run up to Penny Possum to ask her to the dance. But before Penny could say yes, Charles had been lifted away by the bearodactyl and Penny was the only witness.

While that was going on, Johnny the sasquatch, Peter the wolf, and Jason the hockey goalie were wrestling on the ground over who would get to take Petunia to the dance. None of the boys cared that she was half-flower half-girl, purple from head to foot, and was always surrounded by buzzing bees. They figured bees only like pretty flowers, so Petunia must be super pretty.

Petunia ran right past them and hugged Steven Kingsley, the best writer in class, who was holding up a sign written in his notebook asking her to the dance. Since Petunia loved reading his stories, she said yes right away.

Johnny, Fred, and Jason were still busy wrestling and didn't notice Penny Possum was jumping up and down and waving her arms like a lunatic. Penny dared not speak what happened, because when she speaks, her voice is like a cannon and anyone standing within a thirty-foot radius will get hit by a sonic wrecking ball.

Petunia noticed Penny's desperate signals and broke her hug with Stephen.

"Guys! Look up in the sky!" said Petunia.

The three friends stopped fighting just in time to notice Charles Nukid dangling over the horizon in the bearodactyl's talons.

"Well," said Johnny, "Looks like I can cancel my trip to Bigfoot Country this spring break."

"Tell me about it," said Fred. I was planning on waking up for a few hours so I wouldn't have to keep fighting scary monsters." As usual, Fred thought he was dreaming because he didn't believe in monsters and was sure they only existed in his nightmares.

Jason added, "I was planning on washing the inside of this hockey mask. It's starting to smell really bad."

"That's all well and good," said Petunia, "but that bearodactyl is probably taking Charles to Monster Kingdom across the ocean. How are we supposed to get there to rescue him?"

Steven Kingsley piped in, "Last time, we got to Monster Kingdom by riding on the backs of dragon students from Firecrest Middle School. Anyone stay friends with them?"

They all shook their heads.

"Rats. Me neither. Wait... a boy with a dragon friend? Now *that* would make a good story!" Stephen ran off to go write a story leaving his date, Petunia, in the dust.

Silence, said Penny Possum.

"That's right!" said Petunia, interpreting Penny's silence. "There is one dragon we know."

"No way, no how, not a chance," said Johnny. "Anyone but *him*!"

An hour later, all the friends met up at the Dance of Destiny inside Petrified Pavilion.

The dance was being chaperoned by the two strictest and *hungriest* teachers—Ms. T the T-Rex and Dr. Dragonbreath the ten-foot dragon (he'd grown a foot since Book One). He was always looking for a student to break a rule so he could have a tasty human snack. He was also their only hope of getting to Monster Kingdom to rescue Charles. However, leaving the dance to travel halfway across the world would definitely be breaking a rule, so not getting eaten would be a miracle.

Petunia, Penny, Jason, Johnny, and Fred arrived at Petrified Pavilion with their dates. Fred went with Lindsey, whom he had always regretted not going to the Dance of Doom with after seeing what a great dancer she was. Stephen was still somewhere writing his story and was nowhere to be found, so Petunia went with Jason. Johnny asked Rachael, the tallest girl in the class, which worked well because he was the tallest boy.

I told Penny I'd be her date, but reminded her she wouldn't see me because I'd be invisible. The truth was I went to Monster Kingdom to see what happened to Charles, but please don't tell Penny that because she thought she was dancing with me the entire time.

Ramon the zombie kid showed up with Frank (which is pronounced Rachel). Peter the wolf, the meanest, hairiest kid in class, managed to get a date with Tanya Tarantula, the hairiest girl the class, so that worked well too.

The friends were dancing with each other on the dance floor but were also keeping an eye out for Dr. Dragonbreath, who was nowhere to be seen. That only meant he was hiding somewhere keeping an eye on them.

Petrified Pavilion is not like most gyms. Twisting branches grow high on the walls and torches create frightening shadows and dark crevices. Dr. Dragonbreath was no doubt perched somewhere above them in the shadows, waiting to swoop down.

"Do any of you see Dr. Dragonbreath?" asked Fred in the middle of twirling Lindsey, who was focused on her dancing and couldn't care less about rescuing Charles.

Penny peered upward. She could usually see incredibly well in the dark with her huge possum eyes, but the there were too many hiding spots.

"There's only way to get Dr. Dragonbreath down here," said Ramon. "We have to br–" Ramon's zombie jaw fell off. Frank (which is pronounced Rachel) picked it up for him and helped put it back in place.

"Thanks, Frank," said Ramon. "As I was saying. We have to break a rule to get him down here."

"What rule should we break?" said Johnny.

"I know," said Jason. "How about the no kissing rule?"

"No way!" said Petunia, holding Jason at arm's length.

"Come on!" said Jason. "My lips don't even go through the mask.

"I don't care!" said Petunia. "Not on a first date."

The bees flying around Petunia gathered in formation and buzzed menacingly at Jason.

"Okay, I won't kiss you. Just hold back your bees."

Fred tried kissing Lindsey but she was spinning too fast. Penny tried kissing me but I wasn't actually there. (I was told all about these events afterward.)

Ramon tried kissing Frank (which is pronounced Rachel) but he kept getting smacked in the face by her invisible jump rope.

Rachael tried kissing Johnny but his sasquatch breath smelled like moldy beef and she nearly barfed.

Peter the wolf tried kissing Tanya Tarantula and actually managed to kiss one of her fangs, but nothing happened because kissing giant spiders is technically not against the rules at Scary School.

Petunia was exasperated. "Every second we waste Charles could be closer to being a monster's dinner! We have to do—

Suddenly there was ferocious growl and a girl's scream.

"Get away from me" shrieked Frank.

The group turned and saw that Ramon the zombie kid had a crazed look in his eyes and was snapping his teeth at Frank, who had fallen backward on the ground and was barely holding him off by kicking her legs.

Johnny rushed over and pulled Ramon away. "Not cool!" said Johnny. "Zombies aren't allowed to turn other kids into zombies without permission!"

Ramon looked like he didn't understand Johnny's words. He pounced on Johnny and started gnashing his teeth at his nose.

"No!" screamed Johnny. "Not the nose. It has my freckle on it!"

The students were in shock. Johnny was the strongest kid in class but was losing a wrestling match with the crazed Ramon. Ramon was inching closer and closer to Johnny's nose, about to bite it off, when he was abruptly lifted into the air.

His twenty-foot wings beating furiously, Dr. Dragonbreath gripped Ramon in his talons. Ramon was still desperately snapping and reaching for his best friend beneath him.

"Dr. Dragonbreath lowered Ramon to the ground and pinned him underneath his massive dragon foot, then bared his teeth just inches from his face."

"Biting other students during a dance is forbidden," growled Dr. Dragonbreath. I should eat you right here! Buuuut, Dragons only eat fresh meat and zombies are the farthest thing from that. So I'll let you off with a warning this one time. See, I'm tough. But fair."

"Good work, Ramon," said Jason. "You got Dr. Dragonbreath to fly down."

"What do you mean *got* me to fly down?" said Dr. Dragonbreath.

The rest of the kids were too afraid to speak. Only Petunia bravely stepped forward. "Dr. Dragonbreath," she said, trying to remain calm in front of the angry dragon towering over her. "Charles Nukid was taken by a flying monster after the parade. We think that he's been taken to—

"Monster Kingdom," said Dr. Dragonbreath. "I was worried this day would come."

Fred remembered he was probably only dreaming and asked, "Yeah, so, can we maybe have a ride or something to go rescue him? We kind of owe him after he saved us from that terrible ice dragon last week. And all those karate monsters a few months back."

"You are asking me to take you on a very dangerous mission. But I must admit, I have a bit of an appetite, I mean, soft spot for that incessant rule-follower. So I'll take you on one condition. If we make it back alive, you have to let me eat one of you. After all, I've only eaten fifteen students this year. I'm starting to get hungry again."

The friends looked at one another and realized they had no other option.

"Fine," they said together.

"Excellent. Then let's get going."

Dr. Dragonbreath lifted his foot, allowing Ramon to go free. Without hesitation, the zombie kid lunged toward Johnny, still trying to bite his face off.

"Dude!" said Johnny. "Cut the act! Dr. Dragonbreath already agreed to help us."

But Ramon wasn't stopping.

That's when the giant hand of Principal Meredith Headcrusher reached down and raised Ramon in the air by the collar and held him outside the entrance to Petrified Pavilion two hundred feet in the air.

"Young zombie! You will stop biting right now or I will drop you and it will take weeks to put you back together. Plus, you'll have a week's detention!"

Ramon did not stop.

Principal Headcrusher turned to Dr. Dragonbreath with a worried look.

Then, sounds of moaning and scratching filled the air. It was coming from the school building. The students and faculty rushed to the entrance door of Petrified Pavilion. Beneath them, dozens of zombie waiters from the lunch hall were lurching across the school yard to the massive tree trunk, moaning "Braaaains... Braaaaains."

"Dear heavens," said Principal Headcrusher. "The zombies have turned evil."

3

RAMON THE ZOMBIE KID

AT this point, it's important that you hear the story of a particular student at Scary School who has had many shining moments, but whom you've never learned much about. As you may have guessed from the title of this chapter, I'm talking about Ramon the zombie kid.

What does Ramon look like? Well, all you have to do is look at the cover of the first Scary School book. If you don't have it nearby I'll remind you. He has green zombie skin that's covered in rot marks and decay. Plus, there's usually a part of him that's falling off, like his tongue, his eye, his ear, or his hand. Sometimes all at once.

The cool part about being a zombie kid is that appendages can be reattached and will usually stay on for a couple more hours. If anyone sees a body part lying in the hallway, it's a safe bet that it's Ramon's, so they scoop it up and stick it in his backpack as he creeps by.

Ramon's best friends are Johnny the sasquatch and Peter the wolf. They like to go through Ramon's backpack at the end of the day and reassemble him so he can limp or skate back home.

Ramon was not born a zombie. Neither of Ramon's parents are zombies. Nor are his three older brothers—Hector, Javier, and Pedro. Each of his brothers were actually champions of a different extreme sport before they were even ten years old. Hector was a champion skateboarder. Javier was a champion snowboarder. Pedro was a champion sky surfer.

Sky surfing is kind of like regular surfing, but instead of paddling into a wave you jump out of an airplane with a board attached to your feet.

When Ramon turned seven years old, his oldest brother Hector woke him up and said, "Little brother, I'm taking you to the half-pipe so you can learn to be a champion skateboarder like me."

Ramon was thrilled that he was finally old enough to play a cool sport with his brother. At the top of the half-pipe, Hector said, "Watch close, then do what I do."

Hector dipped the nose of his board down the pipe, gathered momentum, then soared ten feet in the air doing a double twist before sticking the landing and hopping off next to Ramon. "All right, now it's your turn," said Hector.

Ramon was frozen. Even though he was wearing a helmet and pads all over his body, he couldn't bring himself take the plunge.

"What's wrong?" asked Hector.

"If I fall off the board, I could break my neck and die," said Ramon.

"Sure," said Hector. "That's what makes it fun!"

"I can't do it," said Ramon. "Dying would be *no bueno*!"

"Don't sweat it, bro," said his second oldest brother, Javier, patting him on the shoulder. "I knew skateboarding wouldn't be your thing. That's because you're a snow warrior like me. Let's go."

Javier took Ramon to the top of a snowy mountain and strapped him to a brand new snowboard.

"Watch close then do what I do," said Javier.

Javier shot down the mountain with a *whoosh*. He bounced off of boulders, weaved between trees, and soared over gorges. Once at the bottom, he shouted to Ramon, "All right! Now it's your turn!"

Again, Ramon was frozen, and not just because it was ten degrees outside. He couldn't bring himself to take the plunge.

"What's wrong?" shouted Javier.

"If I lose control of the board, I could crack my head and die!"

"Of course! That's what makes it fun!" shouted Javier.

"I can't do it," shouted Ramon. "Dying would be *no bueno*!"

Suddenly, a helicopter lowered down from the sky. Inside was his third oldest brother, Pedro. He grabbed Ramon by the jacket and lifted him into the chopper.

"Don't sweat it, bro," said Pedro, strapping a parachute to his back. "You must be a sky lord like me. Get ready."

The chopper climbed five thousand feet in the air.

"Watch close, then do what I do," said Pedro.

Pedro jumped out of the chopper with a board attached to his feet. He spun like a top and flipped like a coin as he plummeted toward the ground until his parachute opened and he landed safely in a field.

Pedro radioed into the chopper via walky-talky. "All right, Ramon. Now it's your turn."

Ramon was frozen a third time in a row. He couldn't bring himself to take the plunge.

"What's wrong?" said Pedro.

"If the parachute doesn't open, I could splat on the ground and die!"

"That almost never happens," said Pedro. "Besides, that's what makes it fun!"

"I can't do it," said Ramon. "Dying would be *no bueno!*"

"I thought you might say that," said Pedro. "Roberto, push him out."

Roberto the pilot tried to shove Ramon out of the chopper, but Ramon held onto the rails with all his strength and couldn't be budged.

Later that night at the family dinner table, none of Ramon's brothers would speak to him. He had lost all respect. As he lay awake in bed, he realized that he must have been born into the wrong family and decided to run away.

He stuffed his backpack full of food, grabbed his favorite toy basketball, and ran all the way to the city park. Finding his way to the dark basketball court, he started shooting the ball while he thought long and hard about what he should do with his life.

I can't become a basketball player, he thought. I can't even make a lay up. He heaved the ball as hard as he could, but it barely touched the backboard. He was so upset he bounced the ball harder and harder on the concrete until a crack formed. He bounced the ball harder on the crack a second time. "I'll never be any good at anything!" he scolded himself.

That's when a hand burst through the crack and grabbed him by the ankle. Ramon tried to wriggle away, but couldn't. The creature crawled out from the ground, breaking through the concrete with terrifying crackles, until an almost fully decayed zombie had emerged.

"Braaaains," moaned the zombie, flicking its wretched tongue at Ramon's round melon head.

Thinking quickly, Ramon reached into his backpack, pulled out the food, and started stuffing it into the zombie's mouth — chips, gummy worms, old pizza, a can of mushroom soup — but the zombie kept snapping at him. The last item was his father's burrito, which unbeknownst to Ramon was a *cabeza* burrito, which means it was filled with head meat that had some brain bits in it.

Satisfied, the zombie released Ramon, who was about to run away, but then it cried, "Wait!"

Surprised, Ramon stopped and turned.

"Please don't go," said the zombie. "I haven't spoken to anyone in hundreds of years. My name is Winston."

Something about the zombie seemed different, almost kind, so Ramon decided to stay.

"Thank you," said Winston. "Did you know dozens of zombies are buried underneath this court? All night long they moan 'braaaains' with mouths full of dirt. It's so annoying being buried alive."

Ramon pointed to a sign that said, *No basketball at night. It keeps up the zombies.* "I never knew what that meant until now," said Ramon.

"What are you doing alone in the park at night?" asked Winston.

Ramon told him the whole story of what happened that day, emphasizing how he was a total disappointment to his family.

"So if I'm hearing you correctly," said Winston, "all of your problems would be solved if you weren't afraid of dying."

"I suppose you could say that," said Ramon.

Winston thought for a moment. Then he turned to Ramon and bared its rotting teeth.

The next thing Ramon remembered was waking up in his bed back at home with an insatiable hunger for brains.

Unfortunately the doors to his brothers' and parents' rooms were locked so he went outside and started eating as many bugs as he could find. They had small brains but once he ate a few hundred of them he could start thinking rationally.

Why did I just eat all those bug brains? he thought to himself.

That's when he looked in a car's side view mirror and saw that his skin was green, his eyes were bloodshot, and all his adult teeth had grown in. "Oh dios mio," he said aloud. "I've been turned into a zombie! Hm. That explains a lot."

Then he realized, hey, if I'm a zombie, I'm already dead. That means I don't have to be afraid of dying!

He woke up his brothers and after the initial shock of him being turned into a zombie had worn off, they took him back to the sports facilities.

"Time to take the plunge," said Ramon. He grabbed Hector's skateboard, zoomed down the half-pipe, then soared fifteen feet in the air nailing a triple-twist with a perfect landing — a move Hector had never accomplished.

Next, Ramon snowboarded down the mountain next to Javier and beat him to the bottom by over ten seconds!

Then he jumped out of the airplane with Pedro. The rush of wind knocked Ramon's zombie head clean off his neck. He flew through the air, grabbed it and reattached it. But just as he stuck it back on, he smashed onto the ground having forgotten to open his parachute.

Ramon was in hundreds of pieces all over the place. It took his brothers days to put him back together.

Now Ramon was no longer the disappointment of the family, but the greatest sports star of them all. He was a hero to every zombie far and wide. He even became a "dead-on" shot at basketball a rarely missed a three-pointer.

When he went back to the basketball court to thank the zombie who had turned him, he found that the court was broken apart and hundreds of zombies, both old and new, were having a grand time digging through the sandboxes for ants and chasing squirrels up trees.

Winston hobbled over to him. "Hello, Ramon," said Winston. "How do you like being undead?"

"It's fantastic," said Ramon. "But I have a question. How come all of us zombies are only going after bug and rodent brains when there are big juicy human brains out there?"

"That's a good question," said Winston. "Hundreds of years ago when I was a new zombie, I was obsessed with human brains. But now they don't seem that palatable."

"Same for me," said Ramon. "Weird."

Don't worry, readers. You'll learn more about this zombie curiosity in the next chapter.

Since Ramon was a famous zombie sports star before the age of ten, Principal Headcrusher tracked him down and offered him a free scholarship to Scary School to be one of her prized scary kids, which meant she could charge more tuition for the normal kids whose parents pay good money for them to be terrified at all times.

The kids loved having a famous zombie sports star at their school. Frank (pronounced Rachel) was the envy of all the other girls when Ramon asked her to the Dance of Destiny. She almost stopped jumping her invisible jump rope for a second when he asked, but quickly recovered.

When Frank was kicking her legs to stop Ramon from biting her at the dance, all the other girls were whispering to each other, "What is she thinking? How many girls can say they've been bitten by the most famous zombie in the world?"

4

TURLOCK THE TINY TROLL

"Here we are in the Hall of Great Monsters. The skeleton above you belonged to largest sea serpent ever captured."

Queen Stingbottom was giving the newly crowned King Charles Nukid a tour of Monster Castle. It looked like a monster natural history museum. The bones of the 200-foot sea serpent were coiled along the walls of the immense circular hall. Mounted in different parts of the room were many other monstrous skeletons in fierce poses.

Queen Stingbottom continued, "King Zog apologizes for not guiding you himself, but he's afraid that he'll eat you and violate the law against former kings eating new kings."

"Tell him I appreciate it," said Charles.

"I shall. Now, I'm sure you'll recognize these other skeletons from Monster History courses."

"Of course I do!" exclaimed Charles. There was no class he loved more. "That's Borfbock. The mightiest she-troll who ever lived and first conqueror of Monster Kingdom. That's Snoobarf, the monster so foul-smelling, nothing else could live within a hundred miles of him. He had all of Monster Kingdom to himself for fifty years."

"Awoo-aloo!" said Ms. Stingbottom. "The best kings are the ones who know about the kings who came before them. Do you know why?"

"Um, so they don't repeat the mistakes of the past?"

"Exactly!" Queen Stingbottom was so happy she did a backflip, just like in Monster Math class. "I have a feeling you will make a fine king indeed. But now I have to show you the most important room in the castle."

Queen Stingbottom led Charles down a long corridor. Paintings of past monster kings stared menacingly at them as they walked past. Sometimes one would snort or roar.

Suddenly, a zombie in a tuxedo popped out from a doorway. Charles jumped behind Ms. Stingbottom in fright.

"Care for a snack?" the zombie asked, holding out a tray of bugs and worms.

"Oh, no thanks," said Charles.

"Very good, your highness," said the zombie. Charles didn't notice but another zombie with no legs had lurched along the floor and was shining his shoes.

"What can I say?" said Queen Stingbottom, munching on a gooey beetle. "Zombies love to serve."

"I know," said Charles. "Zombie waiters serve us lunch at Scary School. I always wondered about that."

"You're about to find out why," she replied.

They reached the end of the corridor and stood before an ominous iron door. There was a skull and crossbones at the top. Written in blood on the walls beside it was: "Do Not Enter," "Keep Out," and "Sorry, I couldn't find a marker."

Queen Stingbottom removed one of the bones from Charles's crown, which he was now carrying over his shoulder. It was shaped like a large skeleton key. She turned the lock and the door opened wide.

"In here," said Ms. Stingbottom, "is the Zombie Control Center."

Charles stepped inside. He found it to be an ordinary empty room. The bare walls were the same stone blocks outside of the castle and the floor was smooth and cold. There was only one object that caught his eye — a white horn sticking out of the back wall in a slot. It was sparkling as if it contained magic.

Next to the horn was a sign marked: *Good*.

Underneath "Good" was marked: *Bad*.

Beneath Bad read: *Zombie Apocalypse*.

"That, King Charles, is a unicorn horn. Given to us centuries ago by the great unicorn Tiberius and installed by King Barzolus Graccholius. Have you studied unicorns?"

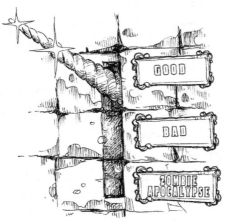

"Yes, I have!" said Charles. "Only one exists in the world at any time. They are usually hiding deep in magical forests and don't like to be disturbed. Their horns are one of the most magical items in the world. But nobody is really sure what the horns do."

"And that is the secret that only monster royalty is allowed to know. Unicorns are the reason that the living and the dead are able to co-exist in our world. The unicorn is an animal of peace. Its horn is like a radio transmitter, sending out signals of tranquility to all the zombies so that they don't devour every human and monster they see."

"Cool!" said Charles. "But how does that horn work if the unicorn it was attached to died centuries ago?"

"Good question," said Queen Stingbottom. "Before he died, Tiberius gave his horn to the Monster King Barzokulus willingly. And when a unicorn does that, the horn becomes more powerful detached than it was on its head. However, if a horn is taken from a unicorn unwillingly, it loses all its powers.

"Before Tiberius the unicorn came along, zombies were uncontrollable, wreaking havoc and zombie-death on humans and monsters alike. The whole world would have turned into zombies if it weren't for this horn in this room. The monster king must make sure that the zombie control horn is always set to good."

"But, why even have the bad settings? And what's the difference between bad and zombie apocalypse?"

"I suppose there are a few cases when the zombies being bad could prove useful. Like if humans changed their minds and declared war on all monsters. We would need the zombies to be bad again to defend ourselves. Zombie apocalypse would make the monsters *so* bad, well, no man or monster on planet would last longer than a few weeks."

"Very, very interesting," spoke a high-pitched voice from behind them.

Charles turned and saw what looked to be a child troll standing in the doorway wearing overalls and a red beanie.

"Turlock? How did you get here?" inquired Queen Stingbottom.

"I'll tell you how," said the troll, "I used my brains. And I've got more of them than any troll alive. Aren't you going to introduce me to the king?"

Queen Stingbottom sighed, "Charles, this is Turlock. Chief of the trolls."

"Chief?" said Charles. "But he's barely taller than me. Aren't grown trolls fifteen feet tall?"

"I happen to be a dwarf troll! But what I lack in size I make up for in smarts. How do you think I got to be chief?"

"Well, you've met the king," said Queen Stingbottom. "Now be gone before I call the guards."

"Ha! Ha! I don't think so. You see, I've been talking it over with the other trolls, and we are none to be pleased with having to take orders from a scrawny human who looks like he couldn't crush a grape."

"Your concerns are understandable, but you should at least give him a chance, shouldn't you?"

"No chances! If he fails, Monster Kingdom could fall to ruin. If he succeeds, Monster Kingdom will be the laughing stock for a hundred years! I hereby challenge King Charles to a duel right here, right now. If he loses, he will have been defeated in battle, and by law, I will be the new monster king. Unless, of course, he's too afraid and would rather give me the crown and spare his body the pain."

Queen Stingbottom looked to Charles. He was no longer hiding behind her, but was standing in front of her, clenching his fists. Turlock's words hadn't frightened him. They had made him furious.

"Very well!" said Charles. "I accept your challenge."

"Then let it begin!" said Turlock. "Since you are the king, you make the first move."

Charles had a secret weapon up his sleeve. His training in Monster Math with Queen Stingbottom had taught him that monsters' one weakness is small numbers. They are afraid of them like humans are afraid of fire. Why? Nobody knows but it probably has something to do with unicorns.

Charles thought of a number in his head and started out with a light jab. "Nine!" yelled Charles.

Queen Stingbottom winced hearing the dreadfully small number.

Turlock flinched, but didn't seem fazed. "Ha! Try again," he laughed.

Charles went in for a heavier hit. "Three!"

Queen Stingbottom fell to her knees in anguish.

Turlock kept laughing. Charles thought he might be wearing earplugs, but they had been conversing normally a second ago.

Charles decided to give him a finishing move. "Negative six!"

Queen Stingbottom passed out.

Turlock smiled. "Is that the best you got? What a shame. Oh, maybe I should have shown you *this* before."

Turlock removed his red beanie and underneath was a pair of monster headphones. "My own creation," said Turlock. "It takes any number that's spoken and adds a million to it. So your silly number tricks won't work this time. Now, it's my turn."

Turlock stomped toward Charles. Even though Turlock was small he was still as ponderous as any other troll. Charles figured his best chance was to use his quickness to avoid him until he got tired and fell asleep.

But then, from behind Turlock, five huge, grown trolls stomped into the room and shut the iron doors.

"This is my army," said Turlock. "Where's yours?"

"Guards!" Charles shouted, but it was no use. No sound could escape the room while the doors were shut.

There was no way Charles could run from all those trolls in the small room for long. He gave himself about ten seconds max before he would be squashed flat as a pancake.

TURLOCK AND HIS TROLL CREW

5

ZOMBIE APOCALYPSE

*F*laring their bulging nostrils and clenching their bone-crushing hands, the immense trolls circled the terrified Charles Nukid at the center of the zombie control room.

Queen Stingbottom remained unconscious on the floor.

Certain it would be his last moments alive, Charles found himself thinking about his best friend, Penny Possum. *If only that bearodactyl hadn't carried me away,* he thought. *If only I had been watching my back like I usually do. I would probably be dancing with Penny right now at the Dance of Destiny. Maybe we would be holding hands, sharing a punch on the roof of Petrified Pavilion. Penny would probably know what to do in this situation. She helped me get out of sticky situations before like when we escaped Mr. Wolfbark and battled the Ice Dragon. What would Penny do?*

In case you forgot, ghosts can read minds. That's how I knew what he was thinking.

"Don't worry. I'll smash him, boss," said one of the trolls. It closed in on Charles with its fist raised high to

37

thump him on the head. As its fist came down, Charles barely rolled out of the way, then noticed a torch on the back wall. That's it, he thought to himself.

But then, another troll grabbed hold of him, wrapping its huge hand around Charles's entire body. But when it squeezed, Charles slipped through its grasp like a wriggly worm. He darted between another's legs and dashed toward the torch. It was too high up for him to reach, so he took off his tie, jumped in the air, and whipped it at the flame.

It went out. The room became pitch dark.

Charles immediately realized this might not have been the best idea. While this would be an advantage for Penny since she can see at the dark, he was just as blind as the trolls and now he couldn't see them coming.

"Boss! I lost him!" grumbled a troll.

"Just stomp around the room and pound the floor. Eventually you'll squash him," Turlock bellowed.

The trolls charged toward the torch where Charles last stood, but he had already crept along the walls to the other side of the room. He could hear the sounds of stone cracking and bricks breaking.

This went on for what seemed like hours, as skinny Charles managed to weave and dodge their wild thumps in the darkness by reacting to their foot stomps and labored huffing.

Eventually, Charles became so tired that he lost focus and tripped over Queen Stingbottom's body. He took cover underneath her and held up one of her lobster claw hands. His eyes were becoming adjusted to the dark and he could make out the outlines of the troll's legs. One got too close and he snapped Queen Stingbottom's claw at its shin, causing the troll to yelp in pain.

"Ouchies! Something bit me!"

The troll stumbled backward holding its shin, knocking over three other trolls. Charles was about to dart to the other side of the room, but ran right into Turlock. Turlock dropped his beanie over Charles like a net and held him in place.

"I've got him in my beanie!" said Turlock. "Follow my voice and finish him off."

Two trolls stomped over and lifted Charles in the air by his arms.

Yummy," said the other. But then, the room lit up with orange light and blazing heat. A fireball had burst through the iron door leaving a large hole. Dr. Dragonbreath, Penny Possum, Petunia, Jason, Fred, Lattie, Johnny the sasquatch, and Peter the wolf entered through the fiery chasm.

Embers burning on his teeth, Dr. Dragonbreath growled, "Drop the boy at once. Nobody tears the limbs off of a Scary School student except for his teachers."

"Let's pull him apart like a wishbone," said a troll.

Three Hours Earlier

How did Charles's friends make it all the way to
Monster Kingdom? Last you read, they were trapped
inside Petrified Pavilion while hundreds of zombies were
crawling up the trunk.

Principal Headcrusher raised her enormous hands to
her mouth, which amplified her voice louder than a
stadium PA system.

"Attention students and faculty. The school's zombie population has turned evil and they are climbing up the trunk of the pavilion at this moment to attack us and eat our brains. Please remain calm and exit the pavilion in an orderly fashion. Then sprint home as fast as you can, lock the doors, barricade the windows, and don't come out until you are notified that it is safe."

"Come on!" said Johnny the sasquatch. "We don't have to run. We can fight them off!"

"No," said Principal Headcrusher. "These zombies are our loyal cafeteria workers. I will not have them dismembered or killed when this is probably just temporary. Do you know how hard it is to find good zombie staff?"

Principal Headcrusher looked below. The zombies were still climbing upward. They would be at the mouth of the pavilion in moments. "Hands up!" she called out, signaling the branched hands of the pavilion to rise upward.

The hands were so big they could hold hundreds of students and entire busses at a time. But when the hands reached mouth level, there were dozens of zombies hanging on that had grabbed hold for the ride up. It wasn't just the zombie staff members. Teachers and students had been turned into zombies. The half-zombie teacher, Mr. Snakeskin, had turned bad. Even Sue the

Amazing Octo-Chef was a zombie octopus in a rolling aquarium!

"Cancel evacuation plans!" yelled Principal Headcrusher. "Everybody head to the bleachers!"

The students screamed and chaos broke out.

Zombies were running amok inside Petrified Pavilion and the ones climbing up the trunk were beginning to enter as well. Hundreds of students were fleeing for their lives while the teachers did their best to stop the children from being bitten, only to end up being bitten themselves.

Mr. Grump turned into a zombie elephant-man, but then he forgot he was a zombie and started running from the other zombies.

Lattie the ninja girl was doing flips over the zombies and kicking them to the ground to save other students in peril. She wished she could use her sais on them, but she followed the principal's orders not to injure or kill them.

"Over here, children!" echoed the booming voice of Dr. Dragonbreath.

Usually no kid would go within ten feet of Dr. Dragonbreath, but right now he was their only hope.

Petunia, Penny, Jason, Fred, Johnny, Lattie, and many other students gathered behind him. He spread his wide dragon wings and sprayed a wall of fire that pushed the zombies backward.

Dr. Dragonbreath was about to blow more fire, but instead he let out a loud belch. His stomach started rumbling and bulging.

"Oh no..." said Dr. Dragonbreath. "Not now."

Suddenly, the fifteen students he had eaten on the first day of class nine months ago had been turned into baby dragons inside his stomach and were rolling out of his mouth one by one in balls of slimy goo.

"Awesome!" said one of the newborn dragons. "I'm finally a dragon boy!"

"You'll be a zombie dragon if you don't watch out!" yelled Jason.

The dragon boy quickly realized there was a mass of zombies heading toward him and instinctively blew fire at them. His fourteen brothers and sisters joined beside him and together they were able to create an impassable fire wall.

Principal Headcrusher approached Dr. Dragonbreath. "Why is this happening?" she asked him.

"This has something to do with Charles Nukid. I just know it," Dr. Dragonbreath groaned.

"Charles Nukid?" said Principal Headcrusher. "But how?"

Petunia stepped forward. "He was carried away by a bearodactyl right before the dance. It must have taken him to Monster Kingdom."

"Yes," said Principal Headcrusher, "I have heard rumors that zombie secrets are kept in Monster Castle. Dr. Dragonbreath, will you take Charles's friends there to investigate? I'll work with the teachers to find another way out of this mess."

"Very well. Whoever's coming with me, choose your dragon at once." Penny and Fred hopped onto Dr. Dragonbreath's back.

Petunia, Lattie, Jason, Johnny, and Peter each jumped on the back of one of the newborn dragons.

"Younglings!" bellowed Dr. Dragonbreath. The newborn dragons turned to their creator. "Follow me if a student rides upon your back!"

Dr. Dragonbreath flapped his wings and rose into the air. The newborns tried out their wings for the first time and rose up with him.

"We fly to Monster Kingdom!" Dr. Dragonbreath growled.

Right Now

"Guys!" said Charles. "How did you get here?"

"It's a long story," said Fred. "Whoa. Look at the size of those trolls. This is a really scary dream."

Nobody dared tell Fred he wasn't dreaming for fear he'd lose his courage.

The trolls holding Charles dropped him to the ground. Turlock and his five troll goons faced Dr. Dragonbreath and the Scary School students.

Charles picked himself up and dashed to his friends.

"My army just got here," he said.

Turlock huffed. "Some army! A few kids and a dragon. You sure you want to take us on?"

"Let the boy go," said Dr. Dragonbreath, "if you value your lives."

"That boy happens to be the new monster king," said Turlock. "There's nowhere for him *to* go."

Dr. Dragonbreath and the students looked at Charles in shock.

"It's true," said Charles. "I'm the new king. Heh heh."

"Never mind that!" growled Dr. Dragonbreath. "He's a student of our school and that means he belongs with us."

"Not until I've defeated him and am crowned the new monster king," said Turlock.

"No!" said Charles Nukid. "We can't let him become king. He'd be the worst."

"Then I suppose battle is the only choice," said Dr. Dragonbreath.

Charles looked at his friends. They weren't scared one bit of the trolls.

"Then battle it is," said Turlock. "Charge!" And the fight was on.

With a swift swipe of his tail, Dr. Dragonbreath knocked over the troll leading the surge.

Then Petunia stepped forward. "Bzzz Bzzz!" she spoke to the dozens of bees that were always surrounding her purple hair. The bees gathered and flew right into the eyes of the second troll and stung him all over his face. He fell to the ground in agony.

The third troll was charging toward Jason. Jason tossed up a hockey puck and slapped it with his stick. The puck whizzed through the air and conked the troll in the head. Then Fred leaped on top of the dizzy troll and jabbed him with his long nails. Then Johnny the sasquatch kid leaped forward and tackled him to the ground.

The fourth troll was coming right toward Lattie. "I will bend like a reed in the wind," she said to herself.

Just when it looked like the troll would tackle her, Lattie bent backwards like a limbo champion. The troll's momentum carried him right through the remains of the entryway. As soon as the troll stumbled to the ground, Lattie was on him with a length of rope and tied his feet and legs together so he couldn't get back up.

While that was happening, the fifth and largest troll was heading straight for Charles. Penny saw it getting close. She had been saving her voice all day in case this moment came. She screamed, "Nooooo!" and her voice hit the troll like a cannonball, sending him flying against the back wall and knocking him out.

"Thanks," said Charles.

She smiled, silently.

Turlock was left standing by himself. Dr. Dragonbreath approached him menacingly.

"You know why I'm the smartest troll?" said Turlock.

"Why?" said Dr. Dragonbreath.

"Because I always know… when to run!"

Turlock barreled forward and scurried out of the room and down the corridor in retreat. "This isn't over! I will be king!" he called out as he rounded the corner.

"Well, that takes care of that," said Dr. Dragonbreath. "Now we can get to the business at hand. Charles, something strange has happened at Scary School. You see—

"The zombies," said Charles, with a ghastly look on his face.

"Yes. How did you know?" said Dr. Dragonbreath.

Charles had just noticed that the zombie control lever was set on *zombie apocalypse*. Even worse, half of the unicorn horn was broken off and there was no more magic sparkle to it.

"It must have happened while the trolls were thumping around in the dark," Charles said to the group.

"What is that thing?" said Petunia.

"That *was* the zombie control lever," answered Charles "It kept all of the zombies in the world cool, like our friend, Ramon."

"Not anymore," said Johnny. "Ramon's gone psycho."

Queen Stingbottom woke up from her coma. "Wha-what happened? Did I miss anything?"

She noticed the knocked out trolls and Charles's friends.

"Oh my. I probably did, didn't I?" "Queen Stingbottom," said Charles. "The zombie control lever got set to apocalypse and snapped off. How do we fix it?"

"Fix it? There's no fixing a unicorn horn! It can only be replaced with a new one."

"Okay, where do we find the one unicorn in the world?"

"How am I supposed to know?" she said. "Nobody has seen one in thirty years. But remember if you do find it, it must give you it's horn willingly, or it will have no power."

"Charles," said Petunia. "We don't have time to go looking for a unicorn now. Our friends at school are in trouble. If we can't turn the zombies back to good, we have to return to school and help them."

Charles picked up the crown of bones that had fallen to the floor. He dusted it off and placed it back on his shoulders. He felt a surge of power and responsibility flowing through him.

He looked to his friends and said, "I'm not going back. I am the monster king. This is my home now."

Hearing the moaning and gnashing behind them, the group turned and saw a gang of palace zombies carrying away the troll that had fallen in the hallway to feast on its brains.

6

THE P.E.P. S.Q.U.A.D.

Penny Possum was staring daggers at Charles.

"You don't understand," said Charles. "My people need me. If there's a zombie apocalypse about to happen, I should be the one to lead them. Nobody knows more about zombies than me."

It was true. Charles had been watching zombie movies and documentaries since he was three years old. He understood how they moved and swarmed in groups. He knew what smells and sounds would work as diversions. But above all, he empathized with their condition. Whereas the previous monster king might simply slaughter a zombie horde, Charles believed there was still a soul inside each of them worth saving.

"Dude," said Fred. "I get that it's awesome to be the king, but you're not a monster. You're just an eleven-year-old kid like the rest of us. You belong at Scary School."

"Unthinkable!" said Queen Stingbottom. "No monster king has ever abandoned his brethren in a time of need. He would lose his crown and be hunted for the rest of his very short life."

"Lattie, what do you think?" said Petunia.

"Man will never be free until the last king is decapitated," said Lattie.

"Why did I even ask?" said Petunia, rolling her eyes.

A dozen more palace zombies rounded the corner, moaning and groaning as if starved for brains.

Petunia signaled her bees to attack them, but the zombies couldn't even feel their stings and continued lurching forward.

"Charles," said Petunia, "you have to decide now. We can't hold them back."

Charles looked to Penny. She was no longer glaring angrily at him, but seemed to understand his predicament.

"I'm staying here," said Charles. "If you have to go back, I understand."

"Then I'm staying with you," said Dr. Dragonbreath. "The king will need a bodyguard."

Penny joined his side and took his hand in hers.

"Then it is settled," said Dr. Dragonbreath. "The rest of you return to Scary School. Ride the newborn dragons and bring news of what has transpired."

"Awoo-aloo," said Queen Stingbottom. "But no time to shake claws. It's time to clear a path!"

Stingbottom charged forward, lobster claws pointing in front. She knocked aside the first two zombies.

Jason and Johnny followed after her, tripping them with the hocking stick and tossing them aside with sasquatch strength.

Lattie knocked three away with a spinning helicopter kick and the last ones were taken out by a whip of Stingbottom's stingray tail. Petunia and Fred slid under the zombies' legs and ran as fast as they could down the hallway followed closely by their friends until they reached the courtyard where the newborn dragons were waiting.

"Well," said Dr. Dragonbreath to Charles. "Where does your highness propose we start looking for a unicorn?"

"I suppose the best place is the last place I ever thought I'd go to again. Monster Forest."

Back inside Petrified Pavilion, the fire wall was burning out and the newborn dragons had no fire left. Soon, hundreds of zombies would be upon the remaining teachers and students and the only the only way out was through the opposite end of the massive horde.

"I can't be turned into a zombie," said Wendy Crumkin to Principal Headcrusher. "My vampire boyfriend would think I'm hideous!"

"You probably won't be turned into a zombie," said Principal Headcrusher. "You're the smartest girl in school. That means your brain is extra tasty, so they'll eat the whole thing and you'll be a goner."

"That doesn't make me feel better."

"Well then I suggest you put that brain to use and think of a way out of here."

Wendy thought as hard as she could, but didn't have a single idea where the chance of death was less than ninety-nine percent.

Luckily for her, she wouldn't have to. Within the crowd of students a secret meeting was taking place amongst a very secret club called the P.e.p. S.q.u.a.d. It stood for PEtrified Pavilion's Sneaky Quiet Ultra Agile Denizens. I've been telling you for the last three books that you were going to learn about this club, and now, you finally are.

While most students would swiftly be eaten by the gargoyles perched atop Petrified Pavilion if they tried to sneak in, the P.e.p S.q.u.a.d found a secret way in that nobody else knew about. They would eat lunch in the pavilion gymnasium, hide in her highest branches in times of danger, and arrive early for assemblies to get the best seats.

The current P.e.p S.q.u.a.d members were three sisters Sarah, Lily, and Mia; Chunky the possessed doll; my sister Jacqueline; and the newest member, Tanya Tarantula.

P.E.P. S.Q.U.A.D.

Students always thought it was weird that the members of the Pep Squad were the least peppy girls in the school, but nobody suspected their true purpose.

As you might have noticed, they were all girls except for Chunky the doll. It was supposed to remain an all-girls club, but the youngest members, Mia and Jacqueline, liked playing with dolls and wanted Chunky in the group. They didn't care that Chunky was insane and wanted to kill them all.

Petrified Pavilion showed them the secret way in because the P.e.p. S.q.u.a.d.'s most important job was caring for her needs. They would feed Petrified Pavilion special tree food, massage her branches, and pick off hundreds of bark beetles every day. This kept the tree in tip-top health and her massive mouth always smiling.

Now back to the zombie attack.

In contrast with the hundred of students around them losing their minds with fear, Sarah, Lily, and Mia were standing perfectly still without any hint of emotion on their faces. Each had long straight black hair down to their waists and had long bangs that covered their eyes.

"We seem to be in quite the pickle," said Sarah totally monotone.

"I agree," said Lily in the same monotone. "We could escape through our secret exit, but then our secret passage would no longer be secret."

"It would be the end of our club," said Mia.

"Forget your stupid club!" said Chunky. "We have to save our skins first. And once we escape, I'm going to slice your toes off!"

"You say the cutest things," said Mia.

"No I don't!" said Chunky waving his arms, which he didn't have much control over cause they were filled with stuffing. "I'm twisted and evil!"

"Twisted and evil, yes, but mostly cute," said Jacqueline.

"Argh!"

Tanya squeaked and rubbed her tarantula pincers.

"That's a good idea," said Jacqueline. "Sarah, do you know a spell that would knock everybody out?"

"Huh? Why would I know a spell?" said Sarah.

"Um, because you're a witch?" said Jacqueline.

"Uhhhh…" the sisters stammered.

"Look, the three of you aren't fooling anyone," said Jacqueline.

Sarah, Lily, and Mia thought their secret was safe. Each of them was in fact a very powerful witch, but they were tired of being feared and hounded to do magic at their previous schools. They went to Scary School so they could have a fresh start and be just like everyone else. They didn't even care that tuition would be free if they admitted they were scary kids. They just wanted to fit in.

Unfortunately, they were still so weird everyone assumed they were witches immediately upon meeting them and left them alone for fear they'd be turned into a lizard or a toad if they made them mad.

The sisters had a quick conference then faced Jacqueline.

"Very well," said Mia. "We will perform a spell if you distract the others. We do not believe them to be as perceptive as you."

Jacqueline rolled her eyes. "Fine. Whatever."

The wall of fire would only last another minute at most. Jacqueline jumped on Tanya Tarantula's back. The giant spider leaped to the front of the crowd.

Jacqueline called out, "Everybody listen! Chunky told me he knows a way out. Tell them."

Jacqueline lifted the doll high above her head. Everyone was surprised Chunky actually had an idea. All he ever did was threaten them with ghastly bodily harm.

"My friends," said Chunky. "I may not be flesh and bone like the rest of you. If the zombies tear me apart, I can be sewn back together. But that doesn't mean I—

"Get the point!" yelled Peter the wolf.

"Right. My point is, and I do have one…"

Unseen by the crowd, the three sisters had linked arms and were chanting in a language unheard for hundreds of years. When they finished, a green ball of energy had formed between them and Lily gave a thumbs-up.

Chunky saw the signal. "My point is… I want to gauge out your eyeballs and rip out your tongues! Ha-ha-ha!"

Everyone groaned.

Then the sisters raised their arms and the green ball of energy burst out like a firework. The next moment, everyone in the pavilion, including the zombies, were unconscious on the floor.

"That worked well," said Lily.

"I forgot how fun it is to use magic sometimes," said Mia.

"Time to get to work," said Sarah.

Mia approached a door that everyone thinks is a sports supply room. Indeed it looks that way if it's opened under usual circumstances, but if one knocks three times and says, "Ghuldavia Julmavia" a secret tunnel appears that leads down the pavilion's trunk and exits at the quicksand box in the Scary School playground. And that's exactly what Mia did.

Nobody *ever* went in the quicksand box because they thought they'd never be seen again. Thus, nobody knew it was actually the secret entrance into Petrified Pavilion. The first girl to discover it was named Judith. She decided never to return so that everyone would think she died in the quicksand box and she could start the P.e.p S.q.u.a.d.

For the next several hours, the three sisters dragged all of the students and teachers to the 'supply room' and tossed them down the tunnel. Eventually, they were all lying in a big unconscious pile outside the quicksand box at the playground.

Sarah found Jacqueline and waved her palm over her face to wake her up.

"Well," said Sarah "Everyone is here. Now what?"

"Now comes the real work," said Jacqueline, pulling out a hammer from the tool belt she always kept around her waist.

She walked over to the haunted house she built for me. It took her an entire year to construct it.

"Sorry, Derek," she said. "Your home has to go."

Using the hammer and a crowbar, she began removing all the wood planks from the haunted house until they were all torn down.

Soon after, the students and teachers woke up to discover there were surrounded by a twenty-foot wooden wall that enveloped a huge section of the Scary School yard. The zombies had already woken up and were outside pounding on the walls, but couldn't get in.

"What happened? Where are we?" said Principal Headcrusher.

The three sisters, Jacqueline, Chunky, and Tanya kept their mouths shut. They were good at that. After all, the main qualification for being in a super secret club is being able to keep secrets super well.

"Who cares how we got here?" said Chunky. "You can't survive outside the wall, and you can't survive inside the wall while I'm here! Ha-ha-ha!"

"Mia, please put the doll away," said Principal Headcrusher.

Mia stuffed Chunky inside her backpack.

"Hey! Stop! Aghgh!"

Just then, the newborn dragons swooped down and landed in the playground with Petunia, Johnny, Jason, Fred, and Lattie.

"What happened?" asked Principal Headcrusher. "Where are Dr. Dragonbreath, Charles, and Penny?"

Petunia hopped off the dragon and said, "They're not coming back and the zombies won't be turning back to good any time soon."

"Well," said Principal Headcrusher. "Then I suppose this is our new school for the time being. Don't just stand there. Everyone report to class!"

7

A GORGE OF GARBAGE

Tens of thousands of monsters were once again gathered at the base of Monster Castle. Their newly crowned king, Charles Nukid, stepped out onto the balcony overlooking the crowd.

"King Charles!" shouted a mud-covered monster. "We have done as you commanded and cleaned our caves!"

"It was ten times worse than I thought it would be!" shouted a serpent monster. "You wouldn't believe how much scaly skin a serpent family sheds over the years."

"Me and my buddies collected all the filth and dumped it into Monster Gorge," said a three-headed giant.

"Well done," said Charles, who was flanked by Penny Possum and Dr. Dragonbreath. "I'd like to introduce you to my friends. This is Penny Possum and Doctor… um… I don't know his first name."

"It's Reginald," said Dr. Dragonbreath.

"Really? Okay. Dr. Reginald Dragonbreath. Turlock and his troll friends challenged my position. I battled and defeated them. His friends will not be seen again."

All the monsters pointed at Turlock and laughed. He hid his face under his beanie. Dr. Dragonbreath and Penny looked at Charles strangely. They'd never seen him act so arrogant before.

Charles continued, "Anyone who challenges me will suffer the same fate. Before I didn't know why I had become the monster king and I admit and I was scared. But now my duty has been made clear. My monsters, during my scuffle with Turlock, a terrible accident occurred. It has resulted in all the zombies on the planet turning evil. If you ask Turlock where his friends are, he will tell you that their guts are currently being ingested by the palace zombies and soon they will turn into zombie trolls themselves. I was destined to be your king because I know more about zombies than anyone."

The hairy monster retorted, "But if you weren't made king, wouldn't the zombies not have turned evil in the first place?"

Charles thought for a moment, then said, "Never mind that! Just heed my words carefully..."

The monster crowed became quiet.

"If I hadn't ordered you to clean out your caves, all of you would be zombies already. The number one thing that attracts zombies is a foul odor. They would have been attracted to your caves like flies to a carcass. But because you threw your garbage in the gorge, that is most likely where they are headed. But once they finish there, the will be drawn to the scent of every foul-smelling monster in the kingdom and won't stop until all of you are like them."

The monsters shook with fear.

"What do we do, King Charles?" asked the hairy monster.

"I'll tell you what you're going to have to do. And none of you are going to like it. Each of you is going to have to take… a bath."

"Noooo!" ten thousand monsters screamed at once.

"And not just one bath," said Charles. "Every day you will have to take a bath in the morning and at night!"

"I think I'd rather be a zombie," said the hairy monster.

"That's up to you," said Charles. "But remember, once you're a zombie there's no coming back. You'll lose all sense of self and will slowly decay over thousands of years. All the while driven mad with hunger for brains, even if it's your own family's. I'm afraid that no matter how many baths you take, it will only delay the inevitable. The whole world will turn to zombies unless one thing happens."

"What?" said the monsters below.

"I have to find the only unicorn in the world. It must give me its horn willingly. And then the zombies can be turned back to good."

"You're leaving us, King Charles?"

"Yes. To save you, I must leave you and search for the unicorn. If any of you finds it, for goodness sake, don't eat it or take its horn. Bring it back to the castle unharmed and alert me at once."

Charles and Penny climbed on to Dr. Dragonbreath's back. Charles raised his arms and waved to the monsters below as they lifted into the air. "Goodbye, my people! And remember to bathe! Bathe like your lives depend on it! For they do!"

"We will, King Charles!" shouted the monsters below.

As they soared into the distance, the hairy monster turned to his friend and asked, "What's a bath?"

BATH TIME!

8

THE TEACHER WHO
WASN'T THERE

Principal Headcrusher decided that a zombie apocalypse was not sufficient grounds to cancel school.

Each class separated into groups around the schoolyard ready to begin the day's lesson. Jacqueline's wall surrounding the yard was the only thing between them and thousands of zombies that were gathering, hungry for tender young brains.

Mr. Acidbath's class was sitting around the Well of a Thousand Screams. He said to his class, "I have a very special surprise for you!"

Every student wanted to climb the wall and run to freedom, but then they remembered that zombies would eat them if they tried.

"The Scary School art teacher, Mr. Fischer, will be doing a frighteningly fiendish art project with us today. It's time to see if we have any young Vincent Van Ghosts or Andy Warhowls among you. Heh-heh-heh!"

Petunia was very excited to hear this news. For Christmas she had received a watercolor paint set and had spent many hours painting petunias when she wasn't reading. She ran out of purple paint pretty quickly, but found out she could make more by combining blue and red.

Her classmates were mostly feeling relieved. After all, how dangerous could an art project be?

They were about to find out.

Mr. Acidbath reached out his hand and said, "Class, say hello to your art teacher, Mr. Fischer."

Nobody said hello because Mr. Fischer was not there. They assumed Mr. Acidbath was experiencing strange side effects from drinking one of his potions.

Wendy Crumkin raised her hand. "Mr. Acidbath, there's nobody there."

"Why would you say that?"

"Because there's nobody there."

"Well, I don't see your brain. Does that mean *it* isn't there?" Mr. Acidbath retorted.

Wendy didn't have an answer for that. It was usually a waste of time to get into an argument with a teacher who's a mad scientist.

Mr. Acidbath pulled out a bottle of white liquid and poured a few drops on the ground. The class quickly put on the gas masks that they kept handy in their backpacks. A cloud of smoke rose from the ground.

From within the smoke, a human figure took shape.

The figure lurked across the grass, enveloped by the smoky cloud. The students hoped it wouldn't come near them. Then, the figure stopped in front of Steven Kingsley and pointed a sharp object at his face.

Steven felt all the fear he had conquered before winter break rush back to him and he screamed for his life. Then he realized the figure had merely dropped a paintbrush on his lap. Steven felt very embarrassed.

The figure went around the room handing out art supplies to each member of the class. The smoke disappeared, and with it, the figure disappeared as well.

"Not to worry!" said Mr. Acidbath. "There is one other way you will be able to see Mr. Fischer."

Mr. Acidbath pulled off a trench coat he was wearing. The coat floated in the air and wrapped itself around the figure. Then a hat floated in the air and situated itself atop of the figure's head.

Once his clothes were put on, it was obvious who Mr. Fischer was.

The Invisible Man!

"Good afternoon, young artists," Mr. Fischer spoke. His voice was raspy like a shard of coal was stuck in his throat. "Today is your lucky day, because by the end of class, all of you will have created a masterpiece of modern art. If you don't, I fear you won't be leaving here as alive as you were before."

MR. FISCHER: THE INVISIBLE MAN

The class gulped. Fred blurted, "But I stink at art! I can't even draw a stick figure. Look!

Fred held up a doodle he had done in his notebook that looked like this:

Mr. Fischer examined Fred's doodle and exclaimed, "My goodness! You have created a masterpiece of abstract art! You could sell this for a million dollars!"

"Really?" said Fred, beaming with excitement.

"No! Are you kidding? It's terrible. You have about two minutes to improve tremendously or you're going to be in big trouble. But, don't worry, with the Well of a

Thousand Screams for inspiration I expect all of you will create astonishing works."

The Well of a Thousand Screams is an old stone well with a bucket resting on a rope beneath a conical roof. Kids have sometimes jumped into the well when running away from a gargoyle or a werewolf, but once they went in, they were never heard from again. It is said that once you fall in, you just keep falling for the rest of your life. If you put your ear to the mouth of the well, you can still hear the screams of those who have fallen over the years echoing their way up the stone walls.

It's super-duper creepy.

Mr. Fischer continued, "Because I'm so very famous, I'm sure you all know that I am considered the very best in the world at invisible art."

No one in the class knew he was famous, nor had they ever heard of invisible art.

"I have brought some of my most famous pieces to show you."

Propped next to Mr. Fischer was a painting hidden by a blue sheet. He removed it, revealing a painting of... nothing. It was just a blank white canvas.

"This painting is called *A One-Legged Goblin Dances in the Moonlight*."

It looked like this (turn page):

A ONE-LEGGED GOBLIN DANCES
IN THE MOONLIGHT

There was no goblin. There was no dancing. There was no moonlight.

Johnny raised his sasquatch hand and said, "Hey! Where's the goblin?"

"Why, it's in your mind of course! Whatever image came into your head is what you projected onto the canvas. That's invisible art!"

"Ohhh. Now I see the goblin!" said Johnny, smiling. "Ha-ha! He's hilarious!"

Next, Mr. Fischer lifted a cover off a pedestal. There was, of course, nothing on the pedestal. "This is my latest invisible sculpture. It's called, *The Obese Matador gets Gored by a Bull*." The class laughed and applauded. They could really see that poor matador!

"Thank you," said Mr. Fischer. "I've been working on that one for over two years."

"What took you so long?" Jason asked.

"It's hard carving invisible marble! Have you ever tried to do it? If you think it's so easy, let's see what you can do. Everyone has a half hour to paint a masterpiece or it may well be the last thing you ever paint. And don't be too anxious to try invisible art unless you think it would be as good as mine."

The class got to work on their paintings. A half hour later, Mr. Fischer instructed them to put down their brushes so he could examine their work.

"Who wants to show their painting first?"

The zombie elephant-man, Mr. Grump, raised his trunk. At the beginning of the year he was the teacher, but when Principal Headcrusher realized he literally didn't

73

know anything, she let him stay as a student. Luckily, he still hadn't remembered he was turned into a zombie and was allowed to stay with the class.

"What have you created, Grump?" asked Mr. Fischer.

Mr. Grump help up his painting to show the class. It was a blank white canvas. Mr. Fischer pulled out a long curved dagger from his trench coat. It looked like it was floating in the air.

"Ah. Someone has dared to try invisible art. What's this called?" Mr. Fischer asked.

"I forgot," Mr. Grump replied.

"The title of the painting is *I Forgot*?" Mr. Fischer lowered his dagger. "My word. That's brilliant. Your painting perfectly conveys the blankness of forgetting. I declare this to be a masterpiece. Well done! How did you think of it?

"I forgot."

Next, Jason ran up to the front. As you may remember, Jason is a master woodcarver. He had taken out his chainsaw and carved the wooden easel into a sculpture of his favorite teacher, Ms. Fang.

"Incredible!" said Mr. Fischer. "Creating a sculpture that brings life to a vampire out of the very substance that would kill her if stabbed through the heart. A masterpiece!"

Jason held his chainsaw high and buzzed it with glee.

Petunia brought up her painting next. She had painted a beautiful bouquet of purple petunias growing out of the Well of a Thousand Screams. Mr. Fischer started crying when he saw it. The kids couldn't see the tears, but wet spots were forming on the lapel of his coat.

"Of course," Mr. Fischer blubbered. "You have seen the well for what it truly is — a tomb deserving of beautiful flowers. Truly, a masterpiece!"

Petunia smiled. She hadn't thought of all that meaning behind it. She just wanted to paint petunias and saw the well in front of her. But she was smart enough to act like it was intentional and accepted the acclaim. She was well on her way to becoming a great artist.

One by one, the students stepped forward and their works were miraculously declared masterpieces.

The last to go up was Fred. He was pinching himself extra hard, trying to wake himself up. It wasn't working. Mr. Fischer sharpened his knife on his belt as Fred stepped forward. The class was even more nervous than Fred. They didn't want to lose their class hero. As far as they could tell, nothing had happened that would have drastically improved Fred's artistic ability in the last thirty minutes.

Fred revealed his painting to the class. He held his breath, expecting to feel Mr. Fischer's blade on his neck. He pinched himself over and over, praying he would wake up from this awful nightmare.

His artwork looked like this:

Mr. Fischer proclaimed, "*This* is definitely NOT a masterpiece! You have offended the entire concept of art! Prepare to meet your maker!"

Mr. Fischer was about to slash his dagger, but Fred had been holding his breath for so long that he passed out and fell into a puddle at the base of the Well of a Thousand Screams.

When he fell, the canvas fell over with him and landed in the mud. When Mr. Fischer pulled the canvas out, it looked this this:

"My word. Now *that*," said Mr. Fischer. "Is the most beautiful painting I have ever seen in my life. A museum-quality masterpiece. Fred wins first prize!"

The class cheered, but Fred was still passed out in the puddle and had no idea what was going on .

Later that day, a long line of army tanks rolled through the zombie-infested neighborhood. Inside each of the tanks were the parents of the students.

The students climbed to the top of the wall then dropped down into the tanks, which rolled on back home, clearing a safe path through the fierce attacking zombies.

When Petunia asked her parents where they got the tanks, they responded they were covered by the parents' zombie insurance policies, which they were required to purchase if their kids attended Scary School.

Fred's parents picked up the still-sleeping Fred, brought him home, and placed him in his bed. He woke up just before dinner and exclaimed, "Ha! I knew I was dreaming!"

He didn't notice the muddy painting hanging on the wall behind him with a ribbon that said, *First Prize*.

9

A GIANT PROBLEM

Riding atop Dr. Dragonbreath, Charles Nukid and Penny Possum soared over the cities and towns of Monster Kingdom. The warm sun beat down on their backs and the cool wind whipped their faces.

"See anything yet?" Charles said to Penny, who was peering over the side.

She shook her head.

Soon, they were beyond the boundaries of civilized monster lands and were high above the Wildlands — vast stretches of lawless wilderness where only the toughest monsters dared to dwell. Charles guessed that the unicorn would probably be somewhere in these parts rather than in the cities or Monster Forest where it would certainly be spotted.

"Come on," said Charles to Penny. "You have the best eyes of anyone in the world. You have to see something."

Penny shot Charles a look that said, *bigger doesn't mean better. And they're mostly good for seeing in the dark.*

"Well," said Charles, "keep looking. If you blink even once you could miss the unicorn's appearance. And what about you, Dr. Dragonbreath? Do you smell anything?"

Dr. Dragonbreath grumbled, "Young human, I've never smelled a unicorn before, so I have no idea what I should be sniffing for."

"You've smelled a horse before, right? It probably smells like a horse with a horn. And call me, King Charles, not 'young human.' Respect my authority."

Dr. Dragonbreath huffed. "The only reason I'm not eating you right now is because I'd become the new monster king and I have no desire to be responsible for ruling a bunch of dull-witted future zombies."

"Exactly," said Charles. "It's *my* responsibility. So you'll both listen to what I say or we'll never save our friends or the monsters in time."

Charles pointed to a plateau overlooking a swampy valley. "Land over there," he said.

Dragonbreath landed, gulping air after the long flight.

"This is just a quick break," said Charles. "Let's find water and food before continuing the search."

Dr. Dragonbreath didn't like where they had landed, but didn't want to say anything to upset Charles. All around were caves and waterfalls that fed into the wetlands below. Dr. Dragonbreath found a small waterfall and lapped it up.

Charles and Penny filled water canisters.

Dr. Dragonbreath spat out two wriggling fish at their feet. "There's lunch," he said.

Charles and Penny looked at the fish in disgust.

"What? You've never had sushi before?" laughed Dr. Dragonbreath.

Suddenly, there was a booming voice behind them, "Who goes there?"

They turned their heads but didn't see anything. Again the voice trumpeted, "Be gone! Or suffer the consequences!"

Penny looked wide-eyed at Charles, silently saying, *let's get out of here!*

"No," said Charles to Penny. "Nobody tells the monster king what to do." Charles turned to the direction of the voice. It seemed to be coming from a cave behind a waterfall due to the deep echo.

"Now see here! I am King Charles Nukid, ruler of Monster Kingdom. We only wish to rest here for a few more minutes and then we'll be on our way."

"So the rumors are true?" said the voice. "A human child is the new monster king? Well, no matter who you are, the monster king has no power here. I will crush you as I would any trespasser."

"You would have to go through me first," said Dr. Dragonbreath stepping forward. "Show yourself if it is battle you desire. Otherwise, leave us in peace."

"Very well," said the voice.

Footsteps shook the ground. A shadowy figure lurked behind the waterfall. Then it emerged.

It was nothing more than a little girl. To be more specific, it was a thirty-foot little girl. She had stringy red hair and was wearing a pink parka jacket, black snow pants, and white boots.

DROBNA THE GIANT GIRL

Dr. Dragonbreath, being only a ten-foot-tall dragon, looked up at her in astonishment.

"Ah, I see you're a giant," said Dr. Dragonbreath. "Forgive us the intrusion. We'll be leaving."

"No!" said Charles pulling him back by the wing and turning to the giant. "We are your guests. Will you not follow your monster manners and invite us for supper? We can share with you what we've caught."

Charles held up the two wriggling fish. The giant girl shrieked. "Supper? Those are Scaly and Baily, my pet fish! Put them back!"

"Oh, sorry!" Charles ran them to the pond and dropped them back in.

The giant girl knelt down and pet her fish. "Some guests you are," she said turning to Charles. "You were going to eat my best friends!"

"We didn't know," said Charles. "Do you have anything else to eat? We've been flying all day looking for a unicorn."

"A unicorn?" said the giant girl. She thought for a moment, then said. "Why are you looking for a unicorn?"

"It's a long story," said Charles. "But the lives of everyone in Monster Kingdom depends on it."

The giant girl sighed. "Fiiine. Follow me."

Using Dr. Dragonbreath's wings as umbrellas, Charles and Penny followed the giant through the waterfall and into the cave. Inside it was cold, dank, but enormously spacious. Water dripped from the ceiling in dozens of places. But other than that it was kind of homey. There was a giant rocking chair, a mammoth fur rug (it was literally the hide of a mammoth), an old stinky couch, and even a giant freezer.

The giant girl opened the giant freezer, pulled out a leg of meat, and placed it over a roaring fire burning at the edge of the cave.

Dr. Dragonbreath flew Charles and Penny up to the couch. When the meat was heated, the giant girl set it down on a large plate in front of them. It was bigger than Penny and Charles combined.

"So," said Charles. "You live here alone?"
"Yes," said the giant girl.

"Uh, thanks," said Charles.

Dr. Dragonbreath devoured most of it in seconds, leaving only scraps for Charles and Penny, which was still more than they could eat in a week.

"What for? From my reading I thought that giants lived in large tribes. No pun intended."

"Not always," said the giant girl, not wishing to elaborate. "So why are you looking for a unicorn?"

Charles explained what happened after the coronation and the breaking of the zombie control lever.

"So," said the giant, "you have no idea where the unicorn might be? Not even a hint?"

"No," said Charles. "We were hoping you knew something."

"I was hoping the same of you," she said.

"Why?" said Charles. "What would you need a unicorn for?"

"You really think I want to be all alone up here? I'm still a little girl."

"*Little* girl?" said Charles.

"That's right. I just turned ten a week ago."

The giant girl pointed to a mostly un-eaten cake sitting in the corner that was the size of a shed.

"Oh," said Charles. "I didn't know you were a kid. We're about the same age as you. Where's your family?"

The giant girl began crying tears so big they splashed onto the floor when they landed, spraying Charles and Penny in the face each time.

"They sent me away because I'm a runt. Most girls my age are at least fifty feet tall. I'm only thirty. 'A giant disgrace' they called me. My parents said I need room to grow so they told me to leave and find someplace where there was nobody else around and not to come back until I was the proper height. I've been here over a year and I'm still nowhere near fifty feet tall. But if I can find the unicorn, it will have to grant me a wish. Then I can ask to be normal height and go back to my family."

Penny stroked the giant's enormous fingertip in consolation.

"Penny says she's sorry for you," said Charles. "She doesn't talk much."

The giant girl continued, "I camped out on this plateau because it overlooks the entire wetlands. I spend all day waiting for the unicorn to get a drink down below, but it hasn't come."

Dr. Dragonbreath piped in, "Well, this has been a lovely afternoon, but we should get going before it gets dark."

"Not yet!" said Charles. "I want the giant to come with us."

"Not a chance!" said Dr. Dragonbreath. "The two of you are heavy enough."

"I don't mean for her to ride on your back. We can walk these lands until we find the unicorn. You chose this spot for a reason, didn't you?"

"Yes," said the giant. "This is where the unicorn was last seen almost ten years ago."

"I knew it!" said Charles. "Maybe it comes back to get a drink every ten years."

Charles knew from his studies that unicorns only drink every ten years. These waterfalls had the purest water he'd after tasted. It made perfect sense.

"So, if we find the unicorn," said the giant, "you'll let it grant me a wish before you take its horn, right?"

"Of course," said Charles. "As long as you help us find it."

Charles wasn't exactly telling the truth, but he figured that a king must tell a lie sometimes when it was for the greater good. Charles had read that if a unicorn grants a wish, it loses its powers and the horn would be useless. But he figured he could cross that bridge if they ever came to it. After all, what were the chances of actually finding the unicorn before giving up and flying somewhere else? Very slim.

As Charles and Penny snuggled up to sleep under Dr. Dragonbreath's wing, the giant girl came by and handed them a sliver of her blanket, which was as large as a king-size comforter to them.

"Goodnight," said the giant girl.

"Goodnight," said Charles. "Wait, I don't think I ever got your name."

"My name is Drobna. It means 'petite' in Giant-ese. Scaly and Baily say goodnight, too." She held out a fish tank in front of them. The two fish stuck their tongues out at Charles and made rude gestures with their fins.

"Get your rest," she said. "Tomorrow we find the unicorn!"

10

MS. MEDUSA

A week had passed since Scary School had been barricaded inside the school yard and things were deteriorating faster than rotting zombie flesh.

The main school building was so full of zombies it looked like a piece of candy left on the ground with zombie ants crawling all over it.

Thousands of zombies roamed the grounds and pounded on the walls all day and night.

Ramon the zombie kid was always waiting at the front of the entry gates every morning. His friends Peter the wolf and Johnny the sasquatch would bring him fresh insect brains to keep him strong. They just hoped he wouldn't get too strong and break through the wall.

At one point it rained for two days straight. With no roof over them, all the classes got rained on.

BE QUIET, ZOMBIES!

WE'RE TRYING TO LEARN!

King Khufu's class had to take an ancient history test, but the rainwater smeared their papyrus making all of their writing illegible. Since King Khufu couldn't read anybody's papyrus he assumed nobody knew the answers and everyone got F's.

Petunia and her friends would meet each day before homeroom to try to come up with ideas for solving the crisis.

"Any ideas today?" said Petunia.

"But how would we get past the thousands of zombies?" said Petunia.

"Hey," said Johnny. "I said it was an idea. I didn't say it was a *good* idea."

Petunia rolled her eyes, then turned to Fred, Jason, and Lattie.

"Any thoughts from you guys?"

Fred and Jason shook their heads. Then Lattie spoke, "The mark of a true ninja is when she—

"Forget I asked," said Petunia.

"I have an idea," said Johnny. "Let's go to the school library and research zombies and unicorns."

At the start of class, Principal Headcrusher entered instead of Mr. Acidbath. "Children of Mr. Acidbath's class, I have some news," she said. "Mr. Acidbath had been working on a potion that would change the zombies back to normal. This morning he burst into my office saying that he created one that would work.

Unfortunately, in his excitement he ran off like a lunatic, jumped over the wall, fell flat on the ground, and the potion spilled into the soil. The zombies pounced on him and now he's one of them."

The students slapped their heads and groaned in aggravation.

Principal Headcrusher continued, "So, the bad news is no more Mr. Acidbath. The good news is, there are a few less zombie worms we have to worry about. It wasn't easy finding a substitute teacher to come to a zombie-infested school so I chose the only one who applied. Say hello to your new teacher, Ms. Medusa. Good luck."

The students heard what sounded like a dozen hissing snakes behind them. Ms. Medusa slithered to the front of the makeshift outdoor classroom.

She had the body of a green serpent, with long arms, and a bow and arrow on her back. Instead of hair she had dozens of snakes that were hissing and snapping. She wore dark black sunglasses over her eyes.

"Hello sssstudents," she said with a raspy snake voice. "My name is Ms. Medusa. My ssssisters and I are the last of the Gorgons." "What's a Gorgon?" asked Benny the ice monster.

"I am a Gorgon! I expect you all to be on your besssst behavior. Otherwise thisss could happen to you."

Ms. Medusa took out a large toad and placed it on the desk. Then she pulled down her sunglasses and looked it in the eye. Her eyes glowed white and the frog immediately turned to stone.

MS. MEDUSA

The class yelped.

"You didn't have to turn the toad to stone!" said Fritz. "We would have believed you!"

"Fear not," said Ms. Medusa. "Watch thissss."

Ms. Medusa slithered to the other side of the room, pulled out one of her arrows, placed it on her bow and shot it at the stone frog. As soon as the arrow made contact, it turned back to a normal frog.

"See? Just because something gets ssstoned, it can always get un-stoned with my special arrows."

"No. I don't like looking at zombies. Too ugly. At least in comparison to a beauty like me."

"Hold on," said Wendy Crumkin. "Have you ever tried that on a zombie?"

"Um..." said Fred, "Have you ever looked in a mirror?

"Of courssse not!" said Ms. Medusa. "If I did, I'd turn myself to stone. Granted I'd be one gorgeous sssstatue, but why deprive the world of my perfect features so sssoon?"

"Do you think you might be able to give it a try?" said Wendy. "If it works, it could be the end of this zombie apocalypse."

"Well, I was ssscheduled to catch you up on your ancient mythology, buuut, if it will end an apocalypse, I suppose I can try it on one zombie."

"I know just the one!" said Peter.

A moment later, Peter and Johnny came back holding onto their buddy, Ramon. Ramon was snapping and struggling with all his strength, but they managed to hold him at bay.

Ms. Medusa slithered up to him and removed her sunglasses. Ramon immediately turned to stone. Then she pulled back an arrow and shot him in the chest.

When it hit, Ramon was back to regular old Ramon.

"Oh my gosh," said Ramon. "I'm alive! I don't want to eat brains for the first time in years. Quick, somebody give me a slice of pizza!"

"Hurray!" the class cheered.

Lindsey pulled out her phone and ordered a pizza. Unfortunately when the pizza delivery man got there the zombies attacked him and he turned into a zombie pizza delivery man. Luckily, he throw the pizza over the wall first.

"Ramon," said Johnny, "is there anything you can tell us about the zombies that will help us turn them back to good?"

"Sorry,' said Ramon. "The last thing I remember was going to the Dance of Destiny in Petrified Pavilion."

"That's when the zombie control lever broke," said Petunia. "It must erase all their memories so they don't mind biting their friends."

"What are you talking about?" said Ramon. "Why is the class out here?"

Petunia brought Ramon up to speed on everything that had happened in the last week. Then she told him about Ms. Medusa's ability to turn zombies into stone and then back to their human selves.

"Well, I suppose there's only one way this plan can work," said Ramon. "You're going to have to get all of the zombies' attention focused onto one spot. Then Ms. Medusa will have to pop up and turn all of them to stone."

"But how do we get them to focus on one spot?" said Petunia.

"That's easy," said Ramon. "We just need a really big brain. They won't be able to take their eyes off it."

"Great," said Jason. "Does anybody here have a really big brain they could lend us?"

Everyone immediately turned to Wendy Crumkin, the smartest student in the class. "Don't look at me!" said Wendy. "Intelligence has nothing to do with brain size."

"How do you know?" said Jason.

"Because I'm the smartest in the class. That's how."

Benny, the least smart kid in class, raised his hand. "You can borrow my brain, guys. I don't use it much anyway."

It was true. Benny's not-so-smart moves had caused him to be turned from a human to a vampire to a zombie to an ice monster in the last year.

Jason pulled out his chainsaw and let it whir. He carefully sawed off the top of Benny's ice skull and Fred yanked out Benny's icy brain.

Benny immediately dropped dead onto the floor.

(Don't worry, Benny always manages to find a way to come back to life.)

"We got the brain. Let's go!" said Fred.

"Not yet!" hissed Ms. Medusa. "I didn't come all the way from the island of Cisthene to save the world. I came here to teach! First, your ancient mythology lesson."

For the next hour Ms. Medusa lectured the class on why she and her Gorgon sisters should have been the heroes of *Clash of the Titans* instead of Perseus. It actually worked out well because it gave Benny's brain a chance to thaw and become more smelly. By the way, Benny was still lying dead on the floor and hadn't yet figured out a way to come back to life. It's kind of hard to think when you don't have a brain.

As soon as class ended, Ms. Medusa climbed to the top of the wall holding Benny's brain. She placed it in front of her face. All of the zombies in the school followed their noses and looked up at the brain. Then she moved the brain to the side, revealing her glowing white eyes. The zombies below turned to stone.

"You did it!" said Petunia. "The nightmare is finally over!"

"Follow me," said Ramon. "I'll show which zombies to turn back first. They're my buddies from the park."

The gate opened and Ms. Medusa slithered out with Ramon leading the way. The rest of the class decided to stay back until they were sure it was safe.

"To be honest," said Ramon. "As soon as this is all over, I hope I can be turned back into a zombie. How can I face my family if I'm afraid of skydiving again?"

"You're a strange kid," said Ms. Medusa. "And that's coming from a woman with snakes for hair."

"This is my friend, Winston," said Ramon pointing to his zombie friend now turned to stone. "Turn him back first if you don't mind."

Ms. Medusa raised her arrow and aimed it at Winston. But as soon as she did, a zombie popped up and bit her on the arm.

In the split second that it happened, she had just enough time to notice that the zombie's eyes had fallen out. Thus, it wasn't able to look into her eyes a few moments before. Two other zombies without eyes jumped on her tail and started biting her. She turned and saw three other zombies were biting Ramon at the same time.

The rest of the students locked the gates immediately.

Now Ms. Medusa was a zombie Gorgon. Upset that she didn't have any zombie friends to socialize with, she picked up her arrow and starting shooting each stone zombie and then bit them so they'd turn into a regular evil zombie once again. In an hour everything was back the way it was but now the sixth grade class was once again left without a teacher.

"Oh no. Who would dare be our next substitute if the previous two were both turned into zombies?"

The class looked around in confusion because nobody could tell who said that.

"Hey wait a minute. None of you can see me? Cool!" said Benny. "I've come back as a ghost!"

11

CHUNKY THE EVIL DOLL

Once upon a time there was a little girl named Marnie.

She had a tiny button nose and wispy blond hair that curled above her neck like ribbons on presents.

Even though Marnie was the nicest seven-year-old girl you could ever hope to meet, she didn't have any friends because her parents wouldn't let her have any.

It's not that her parents were cruel, they were simply terrified. Marnie wasn't born with a working immune system. That meant that her body wasn't able to defend itself against germs and viruses, so even a common cold could do her in.

At home she had to stay inside a room that was wrapped in industrial strength plastic. The only time she saw the outside world was through a small window that was welded shut. During the day she would see the other neighborhood children riding their bikes and at night she would watch the stars twinkling. Sometimes she would talk to the stars and imagine that the twinkles were them talking back to her.

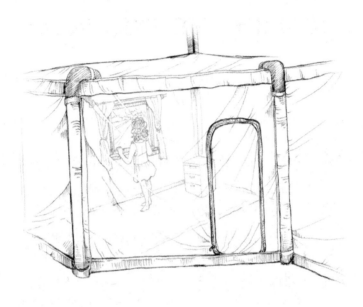

The only other connection she had with the outside was through her tablet computer. When her parents went to the beach, they would transmit their activity through the camera phone to Marnie's tablet.

Even though she pretended that she could feel the ocean breeze, it never felt like she was really there, but it was all she had.

On her eighth birthday, Marnie's parents went into a toy store to pick her out a present.

She made them walk up and down every aisle so she could see every toy before choosing. She decided she wanted a doll and one immediately caught her eye because it was different from the rest. The doll's name was Chunky. It had bright orange hair, overalls, and was, shall we say, a little bit rounder in the middle than all the others. The clerk told her parents that Chunky had been sitting on the shelf collecting dust for years because no kid wanted a tubby doll.

Marnie knew it was meant to be hers. That doll was probably just as lonely as she was.

Chunky was sterilized, brought home, and given to Marnie that night after watching her parents eat her birthday cake. (Marnie could only eat special foods that were pre- sealed in plastic.)

The moment Marnie looked into Chunky's eyes she knew she had her first friend. They played card games together, drank tea together, and watched funny videos together. But no matter how good Marnie's imagination was, she always knew that Chunky was nothing more than a lifeless doll that would never love her back.

So, figuring there was nothing to lose, she decided to wish upon a star for Chunky to be a real boy.

Marnie looked out her window and found the brightest star in the sky. She closed her eyes and said, "I wish for Chunky to be a real, live boy."

Now, if Marnie had wished upon a star, her wish may very well have come true with no complications. However, Marnie did not wish upon a star because the brightest star in the sky that night was not a star at all, but the planet Venus.

Venus is a planet that's hotter than the hottest oven. It's full of sulfur, poisonous fumes, and deadly lava. When you wish upon an awful planet like that, only bad things can happen. That's why it pays to study your astronomy in school.

Later that night, the Venus Godmother appeared in Marnie's window. She looked like a red bulgy devil with tiny wings, and had a pitchfork instead of a wand. She poked the pitchfork on Chunky's heart and said, "You are now a child of Venus. Wake up!"

Chunky's eyes flew open.

The Venus Godmother leaned in, whispered something in Chunky's ear, then flew away.

When Marnie woke up the next morning, Chunky was directly above her, glaring at her with red glowing eyes.

"Rise and shine!" said Chunky. "Or I'm gonna tear your eyelids off!"

Chunky grabbed onto Marnie's eyelids, but she pushed him away before he could do anything.

"Chunky? You're alive?"

"That's right!" said Chunky. "But *you* won't be for much longer!"

Chunky pulled out a sharp safety pin and started chasing Marnie around the room, jabbing at her and cackling.

Hearing Marnie's screams, her parents came in and saw what was happening.

"Hm," said her mother. "I guess that's why nobody wanted that doll."

After Marnie realized that Chunky couldn't actually do any worse than give her a scratch, she was able to subdue him and tied him to a chair using tape and yarn.

"Untie me!" Chunky begged. "I promise I won't hurt you. I'll just murder you!"

Even though Chunky's rampage was the most frightening thing that had ever happened to her, Marnie felt more alive than she ever had.

That night she started researching schools and found an online application for Scary School. No other school would accept her because they didn't want a child who could die at any moment. Children dying wasn't that big a deal at Scary School so it seemed like the perfect fit.

A few weeks later there was a knock at the door. Her mom opened it to find Mrs. T the T-Rex standing there.

"Hello, deary," said Mrs. T wearing her trademark blue dress and speaking in her grandmotherly voice. "I'm here to interview Marnie for Scary School admissions."

Her mom wasn't dumb enough to say no to a thirty-foot T-Rex and invited her in.

Marnie saw Mrs. T and didn't even flinch.

"You're not afraid of me?" inquired Mrs. T.

"Germs are what can kill me," said Marnie. "I'm afraid of small things. Not big things."

Marnie went on to explain that she was tired of living in a bubble and would rather risk her life at Scary School where she would have a chance to make friends.

"Well," said Mrs. T, "the good news is that at Scary School, if you happen to die, that's no excuse for missing class. Not when you can be turned into a zombie, vampire, or some other horrible monster of your choosing."

"I kind of want to stay a human girl," said Marnie.

"In that case we'll have to make a special suit for you. Our science teacher Mr. Acidbath would know how."

Chunky bit the tape around his mouth off and screamed, "Hey you big ugly dinosaur! Aren't you supposed to be extinct? Come over here and I'll correct the mistake!"

"What in the world is that?" asked Mrs. T.

"That's my doll, Chunky. He's pure evil. I was going to get rid of him, but then I realized it's not his fault he's evil. I'm the one who wished upon Venus. So I take care of him and hope he'll be able to be good one day."

"You know why T-Rexes have such tiny arms?" said Chunky. "So their brains don't feel left out! Ha-ha-ha!"

"Well, deary," said Mrs. T. "I think you're the bravest, most compassionate girl I've ever met. I'll be recommending you for immediate admission."

Marnie smiled bigger than she ever had.

Chunky started whimpering. Marnie had never heard him cry before. "Does… does that mean you're leaving me?"

"While I'm at school. Yes."

"But what will I do all day? Who will be here for me to threaten and try to maim? Please don't leave me all alone. I want to kill you. Do you understand? I want to murder you sooo much."

That's when Marnie realized that deep down Chunky was still the same doll that played with her every day and kept her company at night. Curses and threats were actually his way of saying that he loved her.

She said to Mrs. T, "Is there are way Chunky could go to Scary School also?"

"Well, deary, we certainly don't have any possessed doll students, so I'm sure Principal Headcrusher would be interested."

Two weeks later Marnie showed up at Scary School in an orange hazmat suit with an air filter on her face that kept out all germs.

Her classmates had no idea what she looked like inside the suit and assumed she was a hideous creature. That made her one of the most popular girls in the third grade.

Chunky also went to school with her every day and stood right by her side as they entered the school.

Whenever he calls Marnie 'dead meat' or jabs her with a pencil, she picks him up, gives him a great big hug and says, "I love you, too."

HI! MY NAME IS MARNIE.

12

THE SWAMP OF CATASTROPHE

The air was as thick as molasses and the odor more rancid than a thousand rotten eggs.

Charles, Penny, Dr. Dragonbreath, and Drobna the giant were trudging through the swampy marshes in search of the elusive unicorn. With each step, their feet sank ankle-deep in tarry muck.

Charles had to pull his leg out with his hands just to keep moving forward. His mood grew worse every second.

Penny, Dr. Dragonbreath, and Drobna were faring no better. To make matters worse, bloodsucking leeches were attaching themselves to their exposed skin and it was agony pulling each one off.

"Man, this place stinks," said Charles.

"I agree," said Dr. Dragonbreath. "It's quite possibly the foulest place I've ever encountered."

"Duh! Why do you think I set up camp on the mountaintop?" said Drobna. "My feet are sinking, like, ten feet down, where it's even grosser and colder. So I don't want to hear any of you complaining. By the way, thank you, Penny, for not complaining."

Drobna had no idea Penny was silently complaining the whole time.

"Why would a unicorn ever want to come here?" said Dr. Dragonbreath.

"Because nobody else will," said Charles. "It thinks it will go unseen."

Charles looked around. Nothing but mossy trees, reeds, and dirty water in all directions.

"I need a better view," said Charles. "I'll never see the unicorn from down here. Drobna, will you carry me on your shoulders?"

"Not a chance! It's hard enough to walk as it is. Don't worry, I'll tell you if I see the unicorn."

"I don't want you tell me. I want to spot it for myself. Now please lift me on your shoulders."

Penny socked Charles on the shoulder and glared silently, implying, *You just want to get out of the mud and leeches. That's not fair.*

"Don't tell me what's fair," said Charles. "I'm the monster king. I'm supposed to be carried everywhere I go."

Penny rolled her eyes.

"See? No respect!" said Charles. "Other monster kings would have thrown you into the dungeons."

"Enough of this," said Dr. Dragonbreath. "I'm going to fly above the trees and find a place where we can set up camp and rest."

"Don't you dare!" said Charles. "If the unicorn is out there, don't you think it would notice a green dragon in the sky? It would see you from miles away and be gone for good. Our only chance is to spot it before it spots us. Speaking of which, this is your last chance, Drobna. As your king, I order you to carry me on your shoulders."

Drobna gritted her teeth. "Very well, your highness."

She picked up Charles and placed him on her shoulder like a parrot. The extra weight made her sink deeper into the mud. The stench in the air became fouler.

"There's a glade to the Northeast," said Charles, pointing. "Take us there."

"Yes, your highness," said Drobna.

They reached the glade and stood before an arch of vines. The entryway was covered in thick cobwebs. Etched on an old wood sign hanging from the top was: *The Swamp of Catastrophe. No Trespassing.*

"I've heard of this place," said Drobna. "There are stories in giant legends. Only bad things happen if you enter. Not just bad things. Catastrophes. Entire tribes lost or driven to madness. We have to find another way."

"Are you crazy?" said Charles. "If I were a unicorn that's exactly where I'd be—a place where no one would dare to enter."

"But, the stories," Drobna repeated.

"Relax, those are all just made-up legends to scare children. I'm sure the four of us will be fine."

None of the others were as confident as Charles. They were unconsciously inching backward as Charles climbed down from Drobna and approached the cobweb. He felt it. It was as strong as netting.

Charles turned. "Dr. Dragonbreath, if you'd please."

Dr. Dragonbreath stepped forward, reached out one of his claws, and sliced an opening in the middle of the webbing. The stench that emerged made them all start choking and hacking.

"I've smelled the worst things on this Earth, and nothing compares to that," said Dr. Dragonbreath through his coughs. "Whatever is causing that foulness is not worth exploring."

"Have you ever thought that maybe a unicorn makes that stench to scare away intruders, like a skunk?"

"I've never heard that," said Drobna.

"There's much more we *don't* know about unicorns than we do," said Charles. "We're going in and that's final."

Every instinct in Dr. Dragonbreath's body was telling him to turn back, but he figured he'd come this far already. He peeled away the rest of the rest of cobwebs. Despite holding their noses, the putrid odor nearly caused them to pass out.

"We'll get used to the smell after a few minutes," said Charles. "Let's go."

Before them was a twisting pathway through a murky wood. The ground was covered in old dead leaves piled a foot high, as if nobody had walked the path in hundreds of years.

Charles led the way, followed behind by Penny, Dr. Dragonbreath, and Drobna in the back.

As soon as they had each stepped through the archway, there was a rustle of wind. The foul odor disappeared. The leaves on the ground in front of them swirled and danced on the air. They formed into the shape of a horse with a horn on its head.

"It's the unicorn!" said Charles frantically.

When Charles spoke, the leafy unicorn looked at them, then took off galloping down the path.

Charles started running after it.

"We can't let it get away!" Charles yelled.But then, Charles heard a scream from behind him.

He turned and saw Drobna halfway buried in the pathway. Penny and Dr. Dragonbreath were holding onto her sleeve.

"It's a trap designed for giants," said Drobna. "The leaves were covering up quicksand."

"You'll be okay," said Charles. "Sinking in quicksand can take hours if you don't struggle. We have to follow the unicorn."

"Please don't leave me! When you're a giant you sink much faster!"

Charles noticed Drobna was sinking swiftly. He estimated it would only be a few minutes before she drowned.

The galloping sound of the unicorn was growing fainter and fainter in the distance.

Dr. Dragonbreath and Penny were waiting for his decision.

"Leave the giant," said Charles. "We chase the unicorn."

13

BRING YOUR PET TO SCHOOL DAY

Even though the Scary School students did an admirable job putting on brave faces, Principal Headcrusher saw that they were getting more nervous each day as the zombie horde outside the walls grew larger.

She sat at her makeshift office, which was a lawn chair next to the Pit of Skarflacc, trying to think of a way to solve this problem. Then she had the perfect idea. "I know!" she said to the toothy hole in the ground, "We'll have a bring your pet to school day. What could possibly be more fun?"

The pit belched, which Principal Headcrusher thought meant it was in agreement, but was actually an involuntary response from the thousands of meals it was still digesting over the last thousand years.

Until she could find a new teacher, Principal Headcrusher ordered Mr. Grump (who still hadn't realized he was a zombie-elephant-man) to watch over the class. Technically he was a student, but he was their teacher last year for a day before Principal Headcrusher realized the students were teaching *him* all the lessons since he couldn't even remember what math was and history had no meaning to him.

Everyone in Mr. Grump's class brought a pet to show. Some of the students who didn't have pets dug up bugs before class and put them in a jar so they wouldn't feel left out.

The three Rachels—Rachael, Raychel, and Frank (which is pronounced Rachel) went up first to show the class their pets. Rachael had a pet turtle named Rachel. Raychel had a pet tortoise named Rachel, and Frank had a pet toucan she named Flappy (which is also pronounced Rachel).

Fritz showed his pet goldfish named Silver, and Jason showed his pet squirrel named Stumpy. He named the squirrel Stumpy because he had rescued it after turning its home into a stump with his chainsaw.

Petunia considered the bees constantly hovering around her hair to be her pets. She gave them names like Buzzy, Bumbly, and Honeypie. Everyone thought that was kind of crazy.

At the end, Lindsey was showing off her pet mouse named Rascal, but unfortunately, elephants are afraid of mice. Even zombie-elephants. When Mr. Grump saw it, he trumpeted his trunk, went stampeding around the yard and then dove behind a hedge. Nobody saw him for the rest of the day.

In King Khufu's class, King Khufu went first and showed everyone his mummified cat named Pakhet, which meant "she who scratches" in ancient Egyptian. She was buried with him thousands of years ago. Did you know that the ancient Egyptians loved their cats so much that they often had them mummified and buried along with them? It's true!

King Khufu's mummy-cat walked around the classroom, trying to meow, but it sounded more like a rake scraping concrete and it kept hacking up dust-balls. The usually serious King Khufu melted at the sight of his cat and clasped his hands extolling, "Isn't she just adorable? No curses for anyone today!"

Next, Tanya Tarantula brought up her pet rat, Webster, named after her favorite book—Webster's Dictionary. Tanya had found Webster in the basement when he was just a baby and couldn't bring herself to eat him because he was so cute. Tanya had already decided to no longer be a creature of solitude, and they keep each other company while Tanya reads Webster new words from Webster's Dictionary every night.

Bryce the hunky vampire boy brought up his Labrador Retriever named Hector. Unfortunately, King Khufu and his cat were afraid of dogs and as soon as they saw Hector, they jumped into his sarcophagus and shut the lid. Neither came out the rest of the day.

Ms. Hydra crawled under a rock when he saw Julian's fifty-foot-long, three-headed snake! (Ms. Hydra had been subbing for Dr. Dragonbreath while he was away with Charles and Penny.)

The snake, named Tootsie Tail, was so long that Julian held one of its heads in Ms. Hydra's class while his younger sister, Sienna, held the middle head in Mr. Turtlesnaps's class in the middle of the hall, and their youngest sister Anabella, held the third head in Ms. Ghoulberg's third-grade class at the *end* of the hall!

Sarah, Lily, and Mia brought their two hens, Marshmallow and Molasses, who laid fresh eggs in their backyard everyday. The sisters used to give out the fresh eggs to their friends for breakfast, but nobody wanted to eat witches' eggs and they usually got thrown at other kids as pranks.

In Ms.Fangs's fifth-grade class, right after Steven Kingsley had finished regaling the class with stories of his pets who were currently residing in the pet cemetery, Ralphie the Troll brought up his pet hamster, which was light gold in color. As soon as Ralphie told the class its name was Garlic, Ms. Fangs became terrified and turned herself in to a bat.

She tried to fly out of the room, but she hadn't transformed into a bat since September and was kind of rusty at it. She smashed into zombie wall and her left fang popped right out of her mouth and Ms. Fangs went back to being Ms. Fang.

By the end of the day, every single teacher had been scared off by the students' pets. Mr. Rockface crumbled at the sight of Jacqueline's lizard and Mr. Turtlesnaps cowered in his shell when he saw Todd's eagle.

Since the teachers were all hiding or catatonic, the students just played with each other's pets for the rest of the day.

They were more than a little concerned that their teachers might not be much help if the zombies ever broke through the wall and attacked.

14

NOT NICE SPRITES

Penny looked aghast at Charles, silently screaming, *What you mean leave Drobna? She's our friend. She'll drown in the quicksand if we chase the unicorn.*

Charles, always able to interpret Penny's silences, replied, "Look, I'm trying to save the entire world from being turned into flesh-eating zombies. I think that's more important than one giant. No offense, Drobna."

"Offense taken," said the giant.

"Think for a moment, Charles," said Dr. Dragonbreath. "All we saw was a pile of leaves in the shape of a unicorn. Don't you think it was a little too easy for what we've been searching for to appear directly on our path as soon as we entered?"

"In case you haven't noticed, we don't have any other leads. We're wasting time. Leave the giant and let's fly after it."

Not me, said Penny silently.

"Are you really going to disobey the monster king?" said Charles.

Penny scowled while silently miming, *You've changed, Charles. That crown has given you a bigger head than you already had.*

"The crown gives me *power*," said Charles. "More than any human has ever had."

Penny contorted her face, expressing, *What good is power if without it, no one wants to be your friend?*

Then she turned her back on Charles and folded her arms.

Dr. Dragonbreath leaned in and said, "I am extremely disappointed in you, young man. Do you even know why I am here now, protecting you? I am here because if anything were to happen to you, I would never have the chance to turn you into a dragon and raise you as my protégé. Our shared passion for rules made you the most ideal candidate I've found in all my years. Instead of being skinny and weak, you would be strong and fearsome. But a true dragon would never leave a friend to die to chase after a fantasy. If you turn from us now, I shall withdraw my oath of protection."

Charles felt a boiling anger inside of him that he had never felt before. "As if I'd ever want to be a big ugly dragon! I may be skinny, but if it weren't for me, you would have both been killed by King Zog's army and the Ice Dragon. *I* saved Scary School two times. Not you. And now I'm the only one who can save it again. You know what? I don't need your help and I don't want your help. You can *all* drown in quicksand for all I care!"

Charles couldn't believe the words he was speaking as he said them, but he couldn't stop them from coming out.

Dr. Dragonbreath blew a stream of fire that purposefully missed Charles by only inches.

Penny couldn't hold in her voice any longer. She turned to Charles and shouted, "You're not my friend! Go away!"

The force of her voice sent Charles rolling backward down the path like tumbleweed until he was out of sight in the murky wood.

Dr. Dragonbreath turned to Drobna and said, "Take hold of my tail. Penny, climb on my back."

Drobna held onto his tail as instructed, then Dr. Dragonbreath beat his wings with all his might. Slowly but surely, Drobna emerged from the quicksand until she was on safe solid ground.

"Thanks, tiny friends," she said. "What do we now? Should we go after Charles?"

"No," said Dr. Dragonbreath. "He made his choice. I'm going back to Scary School where I can be of aid to my true friends. Join me or not. It is your choice. I say there's just as good a chance the unicorn is in our part of the world as this one."

Penny and Drobna nodded. Penny held onto his neck and Droba hugged his long tail. Then Dr. Dragonbreath flew them out of the wretched swamp and set course for home.

Back in the murky wood, Charles was sprinting after the leaf-unicorn. It had veered off the path and was darting through the trees. Charles gained ground and was close enough for it to hear him. "Stop running at once," he shouted. "Your monster king commands you to stop!"

The leafy unicorn stopped in its tracks. Then it turned its head toward Charles.

"Thank you," said Charles. "I have been searching for you for many days. I must ask that you willingly give me your horn in order to save our world from a zombie apocalypse."

The leaves began rustling. The shape of the unicorn broke apart into a dancing whirlwind before falling to the ground. From behind each leaf, a small winged sprite started laughing giddily, then they flew up into the tree tops.

"Ha ha ha-ha-ha! We-e tricked you!" the sprites mocked in high-pitched voices.

"No... no..." said Charles falling to his knees.

He took in his surroundings. He was in a dark ancient part of the wood. The floor was swarming with crawling atrocities. Glowing eyes were glaring at him. He had no idea where he was or how to get back.

15

DR. JECKYLL AND MRS. HYDE

Ramon the zombie kid hungrily snapped his jaws at the worm and beetle heads dropping from the sky into his hungry belly.

Just like every morning, his friends Johnny and Peter were sitting atop the wall feeding the bug brains to their hungry friend. They wanted him to be strong when he finally returned to his old self.

They were joined atop the wall by Petunia, Jason, Fred, Wendy, and Lattie the ninja girl.

"I liked our idea about going to the school library to research unicorns. Any ideas for how we can sneak in?" asked Jason.

"I talked to Mrs. T about stomping a path there for us. I figured she'd want to help since she's our librarian, but she said if a zombie even got one bite on her foot she could turn into a zombie T-Rex and then we'd all be doomed."

"She has a point there," said Jason. "Lattie?"

"A person with outward courage dares to die. A person with inner courage dares to live."

"I agree," said Jason. "Best not to risk anything and stay alive."

"Nobody ever understands me," muttered Lattie, shaking her head.

"Forget the library," said Wendy Crumkin. "I've already read every book in there. There's nothing useful about unicorns or how to stop a zombie apocalypse."

Petunia was staring into the distance with a worried look on her face. Beyond the makeshift school and the thousands of zombies wandering the grounds was the one place she promised herself she would never go back to. She removed the knitted beanie from her head, allowing her long purple hair to fall past her shoulders. Dozens of bees immediately swarmed around her head to collect the pollen.

"There is one place we haven't tried," she said.

She raised her finger and pointed to Scary Forest.

"Are you crazy?" said Jason. "I'd rather take my chances with the zombies!"

"I've been in and made it out," said Petunia.

Her friends gasped. As far as any of them knew, no student had ever gone into Scary Forest and made it out alive. Petunia never told anybody that last year she had done just that.

After discovering that the bees collecting the pollen from her head were flying into a grove and pollinating petunia flowers that turned into half-human half-flower girls, she was almost trapped there, were it not for a fortunate save by the Scary School staff.

"Why didn't you ever tell us?" said Fred.

"It was one of the scariest experiences of my life. Why do you think I came back that day with my hair chopped off?"

"I thought you were just going for a new look," said Wendy.

"No," said Petunia. "The forest can be survived. In fact, it has a way of getting you what you want. I wanted to be popular and have friends. The only problem is, once you get what you want, you may not like the results."

"Children!" called Principal Headcrusher from the classroom below. "It's time to come down and meet your new teacher!"

A few moments later everyone was sitting in their seats as Principal Headcrusher addressed the class. "Please everyone give a warm welcome to this lovely lady who was kind enough to accept the position despite the last two teachers being turned into zombies. Third time is the charm, right? Say hello to Mrs. Jeckyll, a former chemistry assistant to Mr. Acidbath."

A pretty young woman with a bright yellow sunflower in her light brown hair entered the room. Her perfect skin and shining smile made her look like the nicest teacher you've ever met.

"Hello future leaders of the world, my name is Dr. Jeckyll. Are you ready to learn and have fun at the same time?"

Most students would be excited about a teacher who wanted class to be fun, but the leery Scary School students knew that "fun" sometimes meant going for a swim with man-eating sharks. They shook their heads ardently.

"I can see you're skeptical," said Dr. Jeckyll. "School couldn't possibly be fun, right? Well allow me to demonstrate how fun it can be."

She crouched down behind her desk, disappearing for a moment, then reappeared with a box of fresh hot pizza.

"This type of pizza is called Pizza Margherita," she explained. "It is garnished with tomatoes, mozzarella, and basil, to represent the national colors of Italy—green, red, and white. What is this pizza called?"

"Pizza Margherita!" said the class.

"And what are the national colors of Italy?"

"Green, red and white," they said.

"Excellent!" said Dr. Jeckyll. Now each of you can come take a slice of pizza. I told you learning can be fun."

The class rushed up and everyone grabbed a slice of pizza. As they were munching Dr. Jeckyll continued, "Let me tell you a little bit about my teaching method. I don't believe in homework, quizzes or tests because those are *not* fun. Just like with the pizza, you'll be rewarded with treats, prizes, and playtime every time you learn something. Doesn't that sound fun?"

"Yeah!" said the class, totally buying in.

"Fantastic! Let's get started!" She made a swift turn to the chalkboard, but as she did, the sunflower fell out of her hair and landed behind the desk.

"Oops. My sunflower fell. I'll just bend down to pick it up."

She disappeared behind the desk again, but this time when she popped back up, she looked nothing like she did before. She had stringy black hair, rotting teeth, dark eyes, caved-in cheeks and an angry brow.

"Students! Ach! I can't believe I'm teaching again. What a waste of time."

"Dr. Jeckyll? Is that you?" said Wendy Crumkin.

"I don't know any Dr. Jeckyll. My name is Mrs. Hyde. What in the world? Are you all eating pizza in class?! I never! Give it back at once."

She went around with the pizza box and made the students put their half-eaten pizzas back. Then she reached into her bag and pulled out a stack of papers.

"There's nothing I like more than giving a pop quiz! This will show me how much you know about the War of 1812."

"But we haven't learned about the War of 1812 yet," said Wendy Crumkin.

"Is that true?" asked Mrs. Hyde.

The class nodded.

"In that case… you all get F's for the day! Ha-ha! Not only that, you'll have three hours of reading homework to do tonight in preparation for the three-hour test you'll have tomorrow! Ha-ha-ha-ha! Oh look, a sunflower."

Mrs. Hyde crouched behind the desk and sprang back up as the lovely Dr. Jeckyll with the sunflower back in her hair.

"Whoa. I'm feeling a little dizzy," she said. "I guess I bent down too fast. Where was I? Ah yes, we were about to watch a Bugs Bunny cartoon that will teach you about history. So let's… wait, why is the pizza back in the box? I guess it wasn't fresh enough for you? I'm sorry. I'll make sure it's hotter next time."

DR. JECKYLL AND MRS. HYDE

She closed the pizza box and as she did, the gust of air from the box blew the sunflower off her head.

"Noooo!" the class screamed.

But it was too late. She crouched behind the desk and came back up as Mrs. Hyde.

"Where was I?" said Mrs. Hyde. "Ah yes, it's time each one of you to come up and solve a math problem on the marker board in front of the whole class. And if you get it wrong, everyone gets five minutes taken away from recess and added onto homework time."

Suddenly there was a loud cracking sound. The zombie walls nearby were starting to give. Principal Headcrusher and Mrs. T rushed over to reinforce the wall with a merry-go-round and other playground equipment.

"Pay no attention to that," said Mrs. Hyde. "Focus on this Algebra problem I've written on the board."

"We haven't learned algebra yet," said Wendy Crumkin.

"Well then you better learn it fast or no recess," said Mrs. Hyde.

Petunia looked to Lattie sitting next to her. "We don't have time for this," she said to Lattie. "Can you do something?"

Lattie nodded. She pulled out a ninja star and flung it across the room. It sliced the legs of Johnny's desk in half and both he and the desk went crashing to the ground.

"What was that? A practical joker?"]Mrs. Hyde growled.

Using the diversion, Lattie flipped over the front desks, rolled across the floor, slid under Mrs. Hyde's desk and snatched the sunflower. She threw the sunflower like a dart at Mrs. Hyde's head and it stuck right behind her ear.

Mrs. Hyde spun around and her face turned back to Dr. Jeckyll's.

"Well if it isn't my favorite class I've ever taught!" she exclaimed.

Petunia raised her hand. "Dr. Jeckyll, may my friends and I be excused for some, um, private learning time?"

"How wonderful!" said Dr. Jeckyll. "You're so enthusiastic about learning you want to go off and do it on your own? Of course you can go! Just be back by lunch."

Petunia motioned to her friends and they met at the back wall.

Another crack was forming right before their eyes.

Petunia motioned to the bees buzzing around her hair. "Remember when my bees pulled us out of the Room of Fun in Jacqueline's Haunted House?" said Petunia. "They should be able to carry each of us to Scary Forest to start looking for the unicorn. Now's your last chance to turn back."

Jason, Fred, and Johnny all wanted to turn back. But the truth was they still had crushes on Petunia and didn't want to appear cowardly in front of her, so they said, "Of course we're in," though they secretly wanted out.

Wendy Crumkin said, "My boyfriend Count Checkula can sense when I'm in danger, so I'm not worried. You guys know I'm dating Dracula's son, right?"

They all knew because she wouldn't stop talking about it.

After Lattie nodded her acceptance, Petunia signaled her bees.

But at that moment, three zombies burst through the wall and lunged toward them.

The students turned to run, but in front of them was the deadly slayground, filled with hungry alligators, rivers of lava, and swinging ax blades. They didn't know which fate would be worse and were frozen in place.

The starving zombies gnashed their teeth and were about to bite the poor friends, but then Dr. Jeckyll jumped in front of them. The zombies pounced upon her and began biting her on the shoulder, arms, and face.

"Go children! Save yourselves," she cried while being feasted upon.

The friends were incredibly distraught. "No Mrs. Jeckyll! You're the nicest teacher ever!" said Petunia.

But then the flower fell out of her hair and Dr. Jeckyll turned into Mrs. Hyde.

"Don't eat me!" said Mrs. Hyde. "The children are much tastier!"

"Never mind," said Petunia.

"Good riddance to you," said Peter the wolf.

"Petunia's bees arrived, carrying the students into the forest where only Petunia had ever made it out alive. But this time nobody knew they were going there, so no one would be able to save them.

Back inside, dozens more decrepit zombies had slipped through the hole in the wall and lurched toward the unsuspecting students.

16

THE BOG MONSTER

Charles had no idea if it had been one hour or ten hours since becoming lost in the Swamp of Catastrophe. The sticky vines, the slippery rocks, the stinging bugs, and the stinking sludge made each passing moment a nightmare he couldn't wake up from.

After emerging from inside a log he had hidden in to avoid a giant warthog, he found he was back in the same place where the sprites revealed themselves. "I'm walking in circles," Charles said to himself. "From now on I'm going to go against my instincts and make every turn where I think the path would *not* be."

Following this strategy he still couldn't find the path, but eventually he came to a place he hadn't seen yet. It looked like a field of black mud with a pathway of rocks popping up that he could walk across. A thick mist billowed from the mud, making it impossible to see what lay beyond."

"I bet that's where the unicorn is hiding," he said, giving himself bravery. He gingerly stepped onto the first rock, but it didn't support his weight and sunk down into the mud. Charles quickly pulled his foot back.

"That was weird," he said to himself. "That rock felt kind of squishy."

Charles didn't usually talk to himself this much, but he'd also never been alone in a scary place for this long. Talking to himself made him feel like a friend were there with him.

Then the rock popped back out and kept rising. It turned out not to be a rock at all, but a toad the size of a washing machine.

Instead of ribbit, the toad croaked, "Bog."

Then another toad popped up behind it and said "bog" in a higher pitch.

The same thing happened five more times until a chorus of giant toads were croaking "bog" at different pitches, like they were singing a song called Bog.

Charles had no idea what to make of this, so he decided to walk across the mud and avoid the toads. But as he stepped, the mud gave and he fell waist-deep into it.

"Yuck!" said Charles.

"Bog bog bog bog bog," the toads croaked in chorus.

"I'm so stupid," he said to himself. "You were trying to warn me that this is a bog. It's too soft and muddy to support a body."

He tried to charge forward to escape, but was stuck like a mouse in a glue trap. To make matters worse, the effort caused him to sink another few inches so the mud

was nearly chest-deep. "Well, that's just great," said Charles. "The more I try to get out, the more I sink. How about one of you toads help me out?"

"Bog," croaked the nearest toad.

Charles reached for the toad, but it hopped to the side. The effort made Charles sink another three inches so the mud was at his chest.

"Only one thing left to do I suppose. Heeeelp!"

Charles screamed for several minutes. Each scream sunk him a little deeper until he was neck-deep. In moments he would be submerged. Just when he was about to lose hope, his call received an answer.

"What racket is this?" spoke a gravelly voice from the mist.

"Over here!" said Charles. "I'm sinking!"

A stumpy creature emerged the size of a small dog. It was bulgy and oddly shaped like a melting marshmallow. It had six eyes on the front of its head and four large teeth jutting out from its lower jaw. A poof of green mossy hair sprung from its head. Charles prided himself on knowing every kind of monster but he had no idea what this thing was. It looked like the kind of creature a troll would have for a pet.

"What in the world are you?" Charles asked.

"What am I? Some question that is to ask. What about *who* are you, seeing as you are in need of a friend?"

"I'm sorry," said Charles. "If you don't mind, could we make introductions afterward? I'm about to drown."

"What should I care if you drown? Will not change my life one iota."

"You should care because I am the monster king and am therefore *your* king. I order you to save me at once."

"Ha! What kind of king has no friends or servants to help him?"

"A king who... a king who..." Charles was flummoxed and his nerves were causing him to sink even faster.

"The answer is, not a humble one," said the creature.

Charles realized that was a hint. He would have slapped himself on the head if he could lift his arms out of the mud that was now chin-high."

"Please, kind creature. If it's not too much trouble, would you mind assisting me?"

"All you had to say was please."

The creature waddled over to Charles and extended its lower jaw toward Charles's mouth. Charles bit down on the large tooth and the creature slid backwards, pulling Charles free.

"Better for you to climb on my back," said the creature.

Charles held onto the creature's back as it propelled its slimy body across the bog. It was like riding a lumpy couch cushion.

BARRY THE BOG MONSTER

"Thank you. My name is King.. well… you can just called me Charles."

"My name is Barry," said the creature. "Barry the Bog Monster."

"Nice to meet you, Barry. If I may ask, have you happened to see a unicorn anytime recently?"

"Of course I have," said Barry. "What kind of Bog Monster would I be if I didn't know where the unicorn is?"

17

PETUNIAS AND DODOS AND GIANTS ∞ OH MY!

Seven nervous friends stood at the edge of Scary Forest—Petunia, Lattie, Jason, Fred, Johnny the sasquatch, Peter the wolf, and Wendy Crumkin.

"Well," said Fred, "This is either a smart move or the dumbest idea ever."

The trees whispered to one another in the language of the wind. From where they stood, it looked like any other forest, but they expected it would become much trickier once they entered.

"Well, here goes nothing," said Petunia.

"Oh great forest, we seek the one unicorn. Will you please help us find it?"

The wind rose and the trees whispered to one another in busy conversation. As soon as the wind calmed, the trees starting walking on their roots, rearranging their positions into a twisting path.

"That wasn't so hard," said Johnny. "We should have done this weeks ago."

The friends began walking along the path. As soon as they were well into the wood, the trees at the entrance fell on top of one another, forming a barricade that blocked the way out.

"Never mind," said Johnny. "This was a huge mistake."

They continued down the path. Some areas began to look familiar to Petunia and she realized she was near the grove where all the other petunia girls were born. As if sensing her presence, dozens of purple girls popped out from the ground and ran toward her.

But before they could reach her, they were all caught in a fine sticky webbing that filled the gaps between the trees. The trapped petunia girls called out, "Mommy! Mommy! Read to us! Read to us!"

Petunia's friends were totally freaked out.

"They look just like you, Petunia," said Jason. "Should we help them?"

"Just keep walking," said Petunia. "They are what happens when I let the bees collect pollen from my hair and fly to Scary Forest. Trust me, they are not our friends."

"Weird," said Fred.

Soon after they came upon a colony of Dodo birds. Long thought extinct, they had actually been living in Scary Forest for hundreds of years reading textbooks and expanding their intellect. As the students walked past them with astonished expressions, the Dodo birds only offered them a casual glance.

"Hmph," said a an old-looking Dodo, "no smart child would walk through this forest unsupervised. Pay them no mind. They are not as wise as us."

Lattie seemed annoyed and said to the bird, "A fool thinks himself to be wise, but a wise man knows himself to be a fool."

"We're not men, we're Dodo birds," answered a Dodo.

"Indeed you are," said Lattie.

The forest opened into a clearing with three choices of paths before them.

"Which one are we supposed to go down?" asked Jason.

"I say we show no fear and run down a random path blindly!" said Fred.

"I say we follow the moon," said Peter the wolf. "Awooo!"

"No!" said Wendy Crumkin. "We have to use logic. This is clearly some kind of test."

There was an earth-shaking rumbling from behind them. It sounded like monstrous footsteps. The trees scattered, clearing the way for whatever was coming.

"We have no choice but to take Fred's advice," said Johnny the sasquatch. "Run!"

The friends followed Fred, not wanting to turn back and see what behind them. But then they heard a voice cry out, "Wait!"

They turned and saw a thirty-foot giant girl standing in the clearing.

"What's up?" said the Drobna. "Do you know you're way around here? We're totally lost."

The students stared up at her slack-jawed.

"Wow," said Johnny to Peter. "That's the tallest girl I've ever seen. She's like, twenty-five feet taller than Rachael."

Dr. Dragonbreath and Penny appeared from behind her.

Dr. Dragonbreath grumbled, "Oh, it's the students from the *other* class. Too bad. I was hoping for a light snack, but Mr. Acidbath would be so upset if I ate one of his pupils without his permission."

"Actually," said Fred, "Mr. Acidbath and all of his substitutes have been turned into zombies, so technically we don't have a teacher right now."

"Why would you tell him that?!" said Jason, smacking Fred in the back of the head with his hockey stick.

Drobna kneeled down to be more on their level, but was still twenty feet above them. "Hi, I'm Drobna. Are you guys looking for the unicorn too?"

"We are," said Wendy. "No luck yet."

"Wait, where's Charles?" asked Petunia.

Penny pursed her lips and crossed her arms.

Dr. Dragonbreath answered, "Charles elected to abandon us and explore Monster Kingdom by himself."

"And you left him all alone? How could you? He's our friend!" said Petunia.

"Friend?" said Drobna. "He wanted to let me drown in quicksand."

"That doesn't sound like Charles at all," said Petunia.

"I felt so angry in the moment," said Dr. Dragonbreath. "It seemed like there was no other choice but to leave him behind. I guess you had to be there."

"Wait a second," said Wendy Crumkin. "What part of Monster Kingdom were you exploring?"

"It was called the Swamps of Catastrophe," said Drobna.

"Of course!" said Wendy. "You were probably exposed to swamp gas. Tell me, did it smell terrible?"

"It smelled more vile than a month-old mastadon carcass," said Dr. Dragonbreath.

"That's because swamp gas is a poisonous fume that effects the mind. It takes the emotions you're feeling and amplifies them. Like turning up the volume from one to ten so your brain can't use reason."

Dr. Dragonbreath, Penny, and Drobna hung their heads realizing it was true.

"That does explain a lot," said Drobna. "We were getting along fine until we went there."

"I fear we have made a terrible mistake," said Dr. Dragonbreath. "Charles is still stuck in the swamp. No creature that finds him would allow him live."

18

THE WORMASAUR

"Hot cocoa for you?" said Barry the Bog Monster, handing Charles a warm cup.

Sitting across from the stumpy bog monster on a stool far too small for him, Charles gladly took the cup of cocoa. It had been days since he had any real food and it tasted heavenly.

"Ahhh. I feel like I can think straight for the first time all day," said Charles.

"That's on account of the bog fumes," said Barry. "They make you go crazy of course. Don't you know that?"

"I didn't," said Charles.

"Oh yeah. That's why I spend most of my time in this slightly less stinky bog hole. Cozy, ain't it?"

Charles took in the muddy, mossy walls enclosing a room not much bigger than a school bathroom. The only furniture were a couple of flat stones for sitting and a fireplace. As he thought about the fumes, it dawned on Charles that he had said horrible things to his friends.

"Oh my gosh," said Charles. "I was so mean to Penny. And I nearly killed that poor giant girl. Did the fumes make me do it?"

"Don't blame the fumes," said Barry. "They just nudge you to do what was already in your heart."

Charles grimaced, wondering if he were actually a bad person deep down. He

took another sip of the cocoa. By the way, he said, "I had considered that you might be trying to poison me, but I figured you wouldn't have saved me if you wanted me dead."

"Unless I am wanting to eat you," said Barry.

"Unlikely," said Charles. "I can tell that your stubby teeth are designed for eating root vegetables."

"You got me," said Barry. "Want a steamed turnip?"

"That's okay," said Charles. "If it's not too much trouble, it would be great if you could tell me where the unicorn is."

"In good time. The unicorn is a very busy magical creature. How about some boiled radish?"

Charles stood up, hunching his back because of the low ceiling. "Oh no. You weren't telling the truth, were you? You have no idea where the unicorn is."

"Hey!" snipped Barry. "I'll have you know it's my job to keep the unicorn hidden every time it passes through Monster Kingdom. We're total BFFs. Bog friends forever."

"This is a waste of time. Thanks for saving me, but I have to go."

"Ach! The rudeness! You won't even stay long enough to try my roasted rutabaga? What's so important that can't wait a while?"

"Zombies," said Charles. "They're taking over the world and only the unicorn can stop them."

"Feh," scoffed Barry. "A unicorn gave his horn ages ago to stop the zombies. It's up to the monster king to control them."

"But *I am* the monster king! The horn is broken."

"Ha-ha-ha!" Barry's round body was literally rolling on the floor laughing. "You don't look like any monster king I've ever seen."

"I know," said Charles. "I'm the first human monster king ever."

"Oh really? Then you must know all about—

"The zombie control lever?"

Barry stopped laughing. "How did you know about that? Only the monster king could know. My bog, you are the monster king! I thought you were just saying that when you were sinking so I would save you. I'm so sorry, your highness."

"Don't worry about it. Now will you please take me to the unicorn?"

"Well, since you're the monster king... not a chance!"

"What?"

"The last monster king who met a unicorn convinced her to give up her horn and she lost all her magical powers. And along with it, most of the magic in the world also died. If you take the new unicorn's horn, *all* of the magic in the world would be gone for good. Is that what you want?"

Charles thought hard. He had no idea the world's magic was so dependent on the unicorn. On one hand it wouldn't be such a bad thing if bad witches and wizards like Esmerelda couldn't use magic anymore, but what about the good ones like Marlin the Fizard or Nurse Hairymoles?

"I understand," said Charles. "But if there can't be any more magic in the world in exchange for the lives of humans and monsters, then that's the way it has to be."

"And what if the unicorn refuses to give you his horn? What will you do then?"

"Then I will have failed in my duty as king," said Charles. "I would have no choice but to resign my position as monster king and hope the next king can do a better job than I did."

"You would give up your power so willingly?" said Barry.

"If I have to."

"Follow me," said Barry. "Before you come to a decision that important, you have to see something."

Barry led Charles through the swamp and eventually they came to a pond. Charles jumped in fright. Sticking out of the pond was the head of a giant worm the size of a school bus. It had rows of sharp teeth leading down its throat. Here was another monster Charles had never seen or studied.

"What in the world is that?" said Charles.

"That," said Barry, "is an ancient wormasaur. They haven't existed for thousands of years. This one died many eons ago, but was preserved by the unique chemical qualities of this bog. Over time, the tunnel of its body became something nobody could ever hope to explain. You must enter it."

"Enter it? Why?"

"Because, if you are the true king, you will see the future and know what to do next. But if you are not the true king, you will die."

"Then I have no choice but to enter. For I am the true king."

"We'll see. Good luck, Charles. And in case you are wrong, have a few of my famous broiled beets. Can't ask for a better last meal."

"I'll pass," said Charles.

Barry grimaced.

Gathering his courage, Charles took a deep breath and approached the gaping mouth of the ancient worm. He hoisted himself into its mouth and crawled inside. The mouth immediately closed behind him.

WORMASAUR

19

THE THREE PATHS

The eight students of Scary School, alongside Dr. Dragonbreath and Drobna the giant, joined forces to search for the unicorn. As they reached the end of the clearing, they stood at the foot of three diverging paths that led through Scary Forest.

"Look," said Petunia. "There are footprints on each pathway. But how do we know the right way to go?"

As soon as she asked the question, one of the trees in the forest came to life. A face formed on the trunk, and it approached the group with its roots propelling it forward like tentacles.

It spoke in a deep wooden voice:

Three different pathways, but none have a sign.
Two paths are deadly, and one is benign.
Follow the footprints by hoof or by toe,
Then you will realize the safe way to go.
Choose the right path, you will find what you seek.
Choose the wrong path, your survival is bleak.

The tree then turned around and planted itself back in the forest.

"Did anyone write that down?" said Fred.

Lattie immediately repeated back the riddle word-for-word. The group applauded her.

"How did you do that?" asked Jason.

"Memory is the mother of all wisdom," Lattie replied.

"Look, it's pretty obvious," said Wendy Crumkin. "We have to examine the footprints on each path. There must be a clue in them that reveals the right way."

The friends approached the path on the left. It started straight, then curved into an ominous darkness. The footprints all looked to be made by human shoes. It seemed many people had traveled this way leading into the murky wood.

Next they examined the middle path. It was full of monstrous-looking footprints. There were feet the size of elephant's, and holes in the ground created by long sharp claws.

Dr. Dragonbreath sniffed the footprints and said, "I can smell at least five different kinds of monster feet. Trolls, werebears, harpies, ogres, and cerberuses have all been here recently.

They didn't want to spend another second on that path and sprinted to the third one.

The third path only had the prints of horses, also leading into a creepy dark wood.

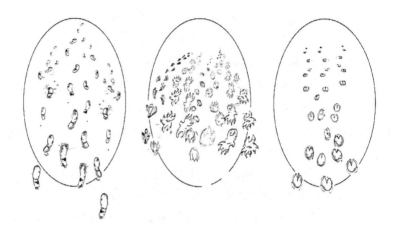

"These are horse hoof prints," said Johnny. "The unicorn is a horse so this must be the path that will take us to the unicorn."

"Not so fast," said Fred. "The first path is the only one humans have taken. Since we're mostly humans here, that's probably the one that's best for us."

Dr. Dragonbreath said, "Are we not going to consider that monsters, with our superior senses, might know the best path?"

"Do you sense anything?" asked Jason.

Dr. Dragonbreath raised his long dragon snout and took a whiff of each path.

"They all smell equally dangerous to me," said Dr. Dragonbreath.

"Then we should probably avoid the path that could be filled with things that want to eat us," said Jason.

Penny ran to the human path and stomped her feet that she wanted to go that way. She was joined by Fred, Jason, and Drobna. They all stomped their feet like Penny. Drobna's stomping shook the ground, causing the others to fall over. Wendy, Dr. Dragonbreath, Lattie, Johnny, and Peter stood at the horseshoe path.

The two groups started yelling at one another. "Don't be fur-brains! Ours is the right path!" yelled Johnny.

"Your path leads only to the afterlife," said Lattie.

The only one who hadn't chosen a side yet was Petunia. She stood between them, still trying to decide.

"It's up to you," said Jason to Petunia. "Come over to the human prints and let's get going."

"Something isn't right," said Petunia. "Both ways seem too easy for this forest. We need to figure it out for sure before we decide."

Petunia took a close look at the footprints on each path again. She looked at the human prints, then the horse prints, then she went back to the monster prints.

She repeated the clue to herself. "*Follow the footprints by hoof or by toe, Then you will realize the safe way to go.* Oh my gosh! That's it!"

"I've made my decision," said Petunia. "I'm going this way." She stood firmly at the monster footprints.

"Are you crazy?" said Fred. "I wouldn't go that way in my worst nightmare, which this might be."

"Come here and look," she said.

The group joined her and looked where she was pointing. Petunia explained, "The human footprints and the horseshoe prints all point one direction—into the forest. But on this path the monster prints point both ways. Monsters have come in and come back out!"

The friends looked at one another in astonishment, realizing Petunia was right. The only path shown to be safe was the one where there was evidence that travelers had returned.

All ten set down the monster path. As they rounded the bend into the darkness, the faces in the trees came to life and whispered, "You have chosen… wisely."

As they continued down the path, they could see glimpses of the other paths to their left and right. They were littered with the bones and rotting carcasses of the travelers that had mistakenly chosen them.

20

THE VALLEY OF THE UNICORNS

After a long hike down the middle path, the group reached a thick wall of trees they couldn't get through.

"A dead end?" said Wendy. "This makes no sense."

Johnny responded, "Or it makes perfect sense if we're about to be attacked by zombies. On guard!"

Then, one of the trees come to life and asked, "What is it you seek?"

"We seek the unicorn," said Petunia.

The trees grumbled to each other and then spoke, "As always, the forest is happy to help."

The trees moved out of the way revealing a cliff's edge with a stunning green valley below.

A wooden sign with words that sparkled in the sunlight read: *Valley of the Unicorns.*

"We made it!" exclaimed Jason. "Hold on, though… Unicorns? There's more than one?"

The group approached the edge and looked down.

Below were hundreds of unicorns of all different colors, galloping across rolling grass hills in magnificent herds.

Most surprising was a giant tree in the middle of the valley that looked like Petrified Pavilion. This one was even larger, sporting the same open-faced screaming mouth at the top of its trunk, and the same long, draping, branchy arms.

Jason, Fred, Johnny, and Peter hopped on Dr. Dragonbreath's back. Petunia, Lattie, Wendy, and Penny climbed onto Drobna. Dr. Dragonbreath extended his wings and glided gently down into the valley. Drobna leaped off the cliff and landed with an earth-shaking thump that rattled the entire landscape.

The unicorns halted in place and stared at them.

"Yippee!" said Drobna. "There are enough unicorns here for all of us to make wishes ten times over. I'm finally going to be big enough to rejoin my family."

A bright pink unicorn cautiously approached them.

"Greetings unicorn. My name is Petunia. We come in peace."

The pink unicorn rolled its eyes and spoke with a young woman's voice, "Whatever, Petunia. Why have you come here? Are you, like, lost or something?"

Petunia gritted her teeth. The unicorn sounded exactly like the girls who were mean to her at school.

"No," said Petunia. "We are exactly where we want to be. What's your name?"

"My name is Shonica. Not that it matters, because this land is only for unicorns. That's what we are. Unicorns. You're not. So you need to get out."

"We won't be long," said Petunia. "We are here because our world is in great peril. Zombies have turned

SHONICA

evil and only the magic of a unicorn horn can make them good again."

"Magic?" said the pink unicorn. "Unicorns don't have any magic. *A-doy!*"

"It's a lie!" said Drobna. "Everyone knows unicorn horns are magic!"

"As I was saying," said the unicorn shortly, "we *regular* unicorns have no magic. Only the great unicorn, Zunicus the Great, can perform feats of magic. He's great."

"And where is this Zunicus?" asked Dr. Dragonbreath, suspiciously.

"Where do you think?" said Shonica. "Up there." It pointed its horn to the giant Petrified Pavilion tree. "I assume you have an appointment to see him?"

"No," said Petunia. "Is that a problem?"

"Um… yeah it is! You think just anyone can wander in and expect to witness the unbelievable mystifying wonder of The Great Zunicus without an appointment? You must be out of your minds. Buh-bye."

The unicorn turned around and started to trot away. The group was at a loss. Then Fred had an idea. "Don't worry, guys. I have experience dealing with snobby girls. I went to a dance with Lindsey *before* she became nice."

"See, I told you," said Fred loudly so Shonica could her him. "The great unicorn won't show us his magic because he doesn't actually have any. He's a total fraud. Let's go back and spread the word on social media."

The pink unicorn stopped and turned. "Ummm… what did you say about Zunicus?"

"That he's obviously a wannabe magic unicorn and can't do anything cool. No worries. We'll be leaving now. Hashtag NoMagicUnicorn."

Fred motioned the group to follow him. Shonica dug her hoofs in the ground and shouted, "Wait!"

Fred turned, pretending to be surprised.

"I guess I can try to see if he'll squeeze you in to witness a display of his awesomeness. But no promises."

Shonica neighed and seven other unicorns galloped to her side. A blue one, a red one, a yellow one, a silver one, a gold one, an orange one, a green one, and a purple one.

"I call the purple one," said Petunia.

The students hopped on the unicorns' backs and rode across the landscape to the enormous tree as Dr. Dragonbreath and Drobna followed behind.

When they arrived, Shonica said, "Cross your fingers that he's in a 'great' mood."

Shonica neighed at the tree and it lowered one of its branch arms and lifted the pink unicorn into its mouth. Then the tree lowered its eyes and noticed the group below.

"Bless my timbers! Humans! Awww, you're so cute." The tree spoke in a nice lady's voice that vibrated like a thousand tubas.

"Whoa! You can talk?" said Johnny.

"Of course I can. Wouldn't be much use for this mouth if I couldn't. Where do you come from? I haven't seen anything but unicorns in years."

"We come from Scary School," said Johnny. "It's near Goblin Hill."

"Well, aren't you a tall bundle of fur?" said the tree, winking at Johnny and tickling him with one of her branches.

"Hey! Cut that out!" said Johnny. "I'm ticklish everywhere!"

LUMBERELLA

Then she looked at Jason and saw the chainsaw slung over his back. "Hey, watch where you point that thing, lumberjack. Not that I'm worried. It would take you about a hundred years to cut *me* down. What's your name? I hope it's not Paul Bunyan!"

Jason just stared dumbfounded.

"What the matter? Squirrel got your tongue?"

"No," said Jason. "It's just, we have a tree that looks just like you at Scary School, but it doesn't talk."

"Oh my gosh! You know Treeanna? She's my sister! I've been worried sick about her ever since she left the valley. How is she? Is she happy?"

"I don't know," said Jason. "She just kind of sits in our yard and lets us have assemblies inside her. I didn't know trees had even had feelings. At least, she's never said she had any."

"Figures. Treeanna was always the shy one. As you can probably tell, I'm the flirt of the family. If you see her, please tell her Lumberella sends her best wishes and misses her so much."

"Sure thing," said Jason.

"You know, we may seem like nothing can ever cut through our bark, but us tree-ladies still need the same love and attention as any other plant. I hope you're taking good care of my darling sister."

Lumberella turned her attention inward. "What's that? Oh goody! Shonica says you're allowed inside. Step on up!"

The group stood on Lumberella's hands and was lifted into her giant mouth.

Inside was the biggest theater any of them had ever seen. But instead of seats, there were dozens of rows of posts for unicorns.

Unicorn guards who were walking with spears in their mouths stepped in front of the group.

"Raise your arms," said the guard in a muffled tone (because of the spear).

The guards searched everyone in the group.

They took away Jason's chainsaw, Lattie's ninja stars, and Wendy's calculator. Then the group took standing-only seats at the front row posts.

Shonica entered the stage and announced, "The Great Zunicus has agreed to show you three exhibitions of his magical powers on the condition that you spread the word of his greatness to your part of the world. Cool?"

The group nodded.

"The let the show begin. Presenting the Great Zunicus!"

Lights flashed and music boomed. There was a burst of smoke, and then, the Great Zunicus, a snow white unicorn wearing a flowing multi-colored cape and sporting a long golden horn, levitated down from the ceiling above.

Zunicus leaped onto a raised platform and announced, "Welcome curious minds, to an experience that will no doubt leave you questioning the very nature of reality."

Petunia shouted, "Zunicus, we do not doubt your powers. We are in desperate need of your help. Could you please—

"Silence human! Once my feats are completed you may ask your questions. But don't be surprised if my answers disappoint you, for a magical unicorn never reveals his secrets."

Petunia crossed her arms and nodded.

"For my first act, I will need a volunteer."

Peter immediately raised his hand.

Zunicus fanned out a deck of cards in his mouth. "Pick a card," Zunicus said with a stuffed mouth.

Peter ran up and pulled out a card. "Now, show it only to your friends." Peter showed them the three of clubs.

"Place the card back in the deck."

Peter put the card back in Zunicus's mouth. Then Zunicus spit out the cards, sending them twirling in the air. Then he stabbed one in the air with his horn. He turned and showed them the jack of hearts.

"Is this your card?" said Zunicus.

"No," said Peter. "It was the three of clubs."

"Oh my! What a terrible mistake! Although, you might want to check your right pocket."

Peter reached into his pocket and pulled out a three of clubs.

"Ta-da!" said Zunicus. "Are you not amazed?"

"Not amazed," said Peter. "I felt the guards put the card in my pocket when they were searching me."

Zunicus started stammering. "Oh.. well.. that's because this first trick was just a test to see if you can distinguish a trick from real magic. I see that you can, so now prepare to be *truly* astonished."

One of the guards wheeled a bushel of hay onto the stage.

"Behold!" said Zunicus. "He waved his horn at the bushel of hay and it began levitating in the air. "Gravity is no match for the power of the great unicorn!"
Lattie, with her trained ninja eyes, could see something barely glimmering in the light. She reached under hear headband where she always kept a hidden ninja star and hurled it above the hay. The ninja star sliced through a length of invisible string, sending the bushel crashing down on top of Zunicus.

"Hey!" said Zunicus, as the bushel of hay burst on his head. "Okay, okay, okay. Those were just warm-ups. Now for the real show."

"Enough!" shouted Petunia. "Great unicorn, we have journeyed a long way because our world has been overrun by zombies. We need your horn to turn the zombies back to good before the whole world is overrun. You might not care about us, but soon the zombies will reach this place, and you won't be able to stop them."

"Young girl, I truly admire your spirit. If I can convince you of my magic, surely I can convince anyone.

Join me on stage and then I'll give you whatever you want."

Petunia sighed, then stood next to him on stage. A guard wheeled out a large rectangular box.

"Please lie down in the box," said Zunicus.

Petunia laid down inside it.

Zunicus picked up a saw with his mouth and mumbled, "Watch as I saw this purple girl in half and then put her back together!"

The group smacked their heads. Instead of purple human feet, purple horse feet popped out the other end of the box.

"I'm all scrunched up in here," said Petunia. "This is really uncomfortable."

"Hey! You weren't supposed to say anything! What kind of volunteer are you?"

"Sorry," said Petunia rolling her eyes. "I meant… I'm really really scared. Please don't saw me in half."

Zunicus "sawed" her in half, pretending to be horrified, then put her back together.

"I am the Great Zunicus! Goodnight and remember to always tremble in awe before me!"

Only the guards clapped their horseshoes together.

Zunicus tried to dash off the stage but Dr. Dragonbreath flew in front of him. The other Scary School kids quickly surrounded him so he couldn't escape.

Petunia squirmed out of the box and approached him.

"I did what you asked, now keep your word. We need your horn to stop this zombie attack, but you must give it to us willingly. Can we please have it?"

"And if it's not too much to ask," said Drobna. "I'd also like to be about twenty feet taller."

"Um… how about NO?" said Zunicus.

"To which?" said Drobna.

"To both your requests! Now be gone!"

"Don't you understand?" said Petunia. "The whole world is at stake."

"Not *my* world, little girl. Why do you think we unicorns came here? So we can live in peace and harmony away from all the horrors the lie beyond."

Penny Possum was beginning to understand what was going on. She had the same feeling back when Mr. Spider-Eyes had conspired with Mr. Wolfbark to fool the students and fix the Ghoul Games.

Penny climbed up Drobna's leg then leaped on Zunicus's back.

"Hey! Get off my back!" shouted Zunicus.

But Penny had already crawled up his neck and was tugging at his horn.

"Stop!" said Johnny. "If we take it by force it won't work!"

At first the horn wasn't budging, but then she realized why. She grabbed hold of it and slid down his snout. The horn slid right off his head. It was tied onto him with invisible string.

"Oh my gosh!" said Petunia. "You're not a unicorn at all. Of course. How could I have been so blind."

"The mind believes what it wants to believe," said Lattie.

"Go ahead," said Zunicus. "Take my horn. It's not like I don't have extras. He buried his head in his cape and turned back with a brand new horn.

"But if you aren't a unicorn, how did you become the "great" one?" said Drobna.

"Fools! None of us are unicorns. We are all horses who grew tired of being worked and ridden by humans as if that was all we were good for. So we painted ourselves bright colors, strapped on these horns, and suddenly everyone thought we were magical creatures and left us alone. We even found this amazing place and painted the glittery sign. When monsters started finding us, they questioned our magic. I knew I had to learn some awesome tricks to fool them. It worked just fine until now. I'm sorry, but you can never leave to tell others what we truly are."

"Look," said Petunia on the verge of tears. "We won't tell anyone your secret, but we can't stay here. The world is depending on us to find the true unicorn."

"I'm afraid we can't take that risk. Guards!"

The group turned to see hundreds of fake unicorns that had gathered in the hall and were pointing their horns at them. Some were holding lassoes in their mouths.

"Though the horns are fake, they still work as spears just fine," said Zunicus.

He stomped on the ground three times and a pit opened on the floor.

"All of you must disappear into the pit," said Zunicus. "How's that for a finale?"

"What's down there?" said Drobna.

"All I know is when someone goes down, they never come back out. I wish you luck. But not really."

"Not a chance!" said Fred. "I'll wake myself up before I jump in." He started pinching himself but nothing happened. "Dang it! I must be in a really deep sleep."

"None of you have a choice in the matter," said Zunicus. "Now!"

The unicorns surged forward. The friends dodged the first few, but there were too many unicorns to evade for long. Dr. Dragonbreath tried to fly away, but the guards threw rope around his wings, causing him to fall like a rock. The rest were lassoed next and couldn't wriggle free.

"Ha-ha!" laughed Zunicus. "We learned *something* from the cowboys that used to ride us."

The friends struggled bravely, but the unicorns charged forward one final time, shoving them into the pit from whence their was no return.

21

THE DEATH OF
KING TOOTHPICK

Charles descended down the throat of the giant wormasaur, gripping the teeth that lined the walls like rungs on a ladder. The further he went, the fainter the light from above him dwindled until he was lost in total darkness.

Charles wondered if Barry the bog monster was telling the truth about seeing his future in here, or if he had just tricked him into becoming wormasaur food.

No sooner did he have that thought than the teeth disappeared and he started sliding down the slimy carcass.

As he slid, the walls of the worm's body started to flicker with bio luminescence. As he gained speed, the colorful lights around him began to take shapes he could recognize. It was like watching a 360-degree movie.

Soon he could tell that it was showing him Monster Castle. He saw himself enter onto the balcony. The imagery was so clear and vivid, it felt as if he were really there addressing the largest gathering of monsters he had ever witnessed. There was unmistakable fear in their eyes.

"My brethren," spoke the Charles on the balcony, "the zombies are upon us. I have tried to find the unicorn that would turn them back to good, but the unicorn remains hidden. We cannot depend on it to save us. We have no choice but to fight the zombies and destroy every last one. The secret to defeating a zombie is this: Do not go straight for the head. That's what it wants you to do. It will bite you when you get close, and even if you succeed in killing it, the bite will turn you into a zombie moments later. The trick is to take out the legs first so it falls face forward to the ground. Then neutralize the neck like it's a poisonous snake. After that, squash its brain by whatever means works best for you."

The monsters cheered in anticipation. "Hail King Toothpick! We fight for you this day!"

At that moment, Dr. Dragonbreath landed at his side with Penny Possum on his back. She had a look of desperation he had never seen before that he couldn't interpret.

"Scary School is under siege," said Dr. Dragonbreath. "Fly back with us and help defend it."

"Go back?" said Charles. "I'm a king in charge of the largest monster army ever assembled. Back there, I'm just another scrawny kid with little-to-no chance of survival. Be gone from here!"

Penny gritted her teeth like she wanted to yell, but pursed her lips shut. She jumped onto Dr. Dragonbreath's back.

Before they could fly off, Charles said, "Once we are victorious, I'll order my monsters to check on Scary School if there's time."

Penny and Dr. Dragonbreath nodded, knowing they would probably never Charles again, and flew away.

Suddenly, thousands of zombies burst through the edge of Monster Forest, groaning and starving for monster brains.

The epic battle began. Charles commanded his army with determined precision. His strategy paid off as the monsters were able to subdue the zombies using his technique. Many monsters were bitten and fierce fights erupted between monsters and newly-made monster-zombies. The casualties on both sides were great, but in the end, the monsters stood victorious over the headless corpses of tens of thousands of zombies.

The monsters raised Charles on their shoulders and together they feasted and sang songs through the night. In the morning, it suddenly dawned on Charles that he had forgotten all about Scary School.

He arrived upon bearodactyl the next day. Jacqueline's walls were torn down and the entire student body and staff were zombies.

"The human world is lost," said Charles to Queen Stingbottom, who was riding a bearodactyl by his side. "Now begins the age of the monster."

MONSTERS VS. ZOMBIES!

The scene shifted to what seemed like years later. Monster Forest had been chopped down to stumps and an enormous wooden wall stretched around the borders of Monster Kingdom to keep zombies out. They built armored caravans and ships that protected them from zombies and established trade with surviving monsters from all over the world.

Within the wall's confines, Charles was revered as a hero. His halls were filled with mountains of gold coins and they built statues of him in all corners of the monster world.   Years later, Princess Zogette left Captain Pigbeard and married Charles. Together, they raised very odd-looking princes and princesses.

More years passed and the prosperity of Monster Kingdom only grew. It had been so long, Charles did not remember the sound of human voices. As he lay in bed, he would sometimes flip through his old yearbooks of Scary School and try to remember what Petunia's laugh sounded like, or Fred's jokes, or Jason's mumbles, but he couldn't. The only voice he could remember was Penny's, whose silence sounded nothing like the shrill, frightening roars of his monster companions.

He so desperately craved the silence, he issued a rule that nobody could make any sound in his presence without his permission. Sound-makers were immediately thrown into the dungeon. To avoid that fate, his monster subjects began avoiding him all together.

When he was sure he was alone, when there was no noise to be heard, he would close his eyes and pretend to dance with Penny at The Dance of Destiny. At the end of the night, he would take Penny to the Scary School drawbridge. She thought it was to feed Archie the Giant Squid, but then he would kiss her as the Archie's peering eye gazed upon them.

When his eyes opened and the fantasy faded, King Charles realized her memory was as fleeting as the silence itself. He pulled his crown over his eyes and cried for the friends he couldn't save from a fate worse than death.

King Charles eventually died, and every monster in the kingdom lined up at his funeral to wish him farewell.

"Goodbye King Toothpick," each monster said as they kissed the face of his sarcophagus, which he had constructed to mimic his old teacher King Khufu's.

He would be remembered as the greatest of all monster kings. He may have gone a little crazy in his old age, but what monster king doesn't? His victories as a child cemented his legacy and paved the way for a world where monsters ruled Earth, where humans were a distant memory, and where there was peace and happiness throughout the land. Or at least the parts of the land that weren't overrun by zombies.

His first-born son, Charles Nukid II, would uphold his legacy, as would the subsequent monster king and queen Nukids for generations after.

As his slide down the worm slowed, the lights began to flicker. Then, as if tugged by an unseen force, Charles shot backwards through the worm like a speeding bullet until he burst out from its mouth covered in slime, landing in the bog next to Barry.

"Well, if it isn't King Charles himself," said Barry. "How does it feel knowing your future?"

The experience was so overwhelming, Charles burst into tears. It was something he hadn't done, even on his saddest day, in many years.

"That's not the future I want," said Charles. "It can't be."

"What was so bad about it?"

Charles pulled himself together and explained what he saw inside the worm.

"Well," said Barry, "if that's your destiny, no use fighting it. Haven't you always wanted to be the most powerful king in history? Hop to it. I'll show you a short cut back to Monster Castle so the glorious days of the monster era can begin."

"Hold on. What I saw wasn't my for-sure destiny, was it? Now that I saw it, it changes things. That was just one possible future."

"It's your future if you follow the path you have chosen," said Barry.

"In what I saw, I gave up looking for the unicorn. But what if I keep looking?"

"About that," said Barry, his pillowy body undulating with nerves. "I have some bad news for you. There is no unicorn."

"What?"

"The unicorn is a myth. Nobody has ever seen one."

"But you said you saw it, yourself."

"That's what I told *you*. In fact, that's what I told everyone. Even my own kin when I installed that phony-baloney zombie control lever."

"You installed the zombie control lever? But that means you're—"

"King Barzokolus Graccholius. Barry for short."

"But that would make you hundreds of years old."

"You know what they say, after your three-hundredth birthday it's all deflation for a bog monster. All things considered I think I still look pretty good for a creature made mostly of mud and gas. I used to be large and mighty, but my body eroded away over time. Someday I'll simply disappear into the bog. When I was defeated in battle I lost my crown and hid myself in this place. My childhood home. It has remarkable preservation qualities."

"But if the lever doesn't control the zombies, why did they suddenly change to evil?"

"King Charles, what I've learned in my many, many years is that the temperament of the zombies is as uncontrollable as the changing of the seasons. Just as the beat of a single butterfly wing can cause a tornado on the other side of the earth, one zombie going bad can start a chain reaction that causes the rest to follow suit. The unicorn horn was nothing more than an old warthog tusk that I carved and had a wizard friend sprinkle magic dust on to make sparkly. I saw that zombies were turning good and wanted to solidify my power by claiming it was all my doing. I made up the story about the unicorn giving me its horn willingly. When I was defeated in battle by the next king, I was so upset about it, I let them keep believing the lie so that they'd want me back when the zombies turned evil again. But it took so long everybody thought I was dead. Now I'm too old and tired to go back."

"Wait a second," said Charles. "Did you say that one zombie turning bad can cause the rest to go bad too? So if that zombie turned back to good, the rest would probably follow him?"

"Yes," said Barry. "But there's no way of knowing which zombie that is when millions have already turned."

"Actually," said Charles. "I have a very good idea of which zombie it is. Would the sports idol of the zombie world likely have such an affect?"

"I suppose," said Barry. "But just what are you thinking about doing? You are destined to usher in an area of peace and harmony for all monsters. Become the richest most powerful most beloved figure in all of history. You wouldn't give that up, would you?"

Charles thought for a moment, but the decision was more clear than anything he had ever known. "Let me tell you something a good friend of mine once said. Well, she didn't exactly say it, but I could tell from her expression what she was thinking. She thought, 'What good is power if without it, no one wants to be your friend?' As I sit here without them I'm realizing that having power never made me as happy as spending time with my classmates. Even if we all get turned into zombies, I'd rather be undead with them than a lonely king."

Barry was so moved, a tear fell from each of his six eyes.

Then, the worm started belching and hacking.

"What's going on?" said Charles.

"I know not," said Barry.

The worm started to gurgle and contort, then ten bodies covered in slime started spewing out of its mouth.

Charles immediately recognized Penny Possum, Petunia, and the rest of the gang. Last out were Dr. Dragonbreath and Drobna the giant.

"We're alive!" said Jason.

"Duh," said Fred. "If we had died, I would have woken up by now."

They saw Charles standing there in his kingly costume beaming back at them.

"Oh, we're back here," said Dr. Dragonbreath. "Hop on my back, children. I know the way back to Scary

School. I'm sure Charles is still too busy searching for the unicorn to care about his friends."

"Wait," said Charles.

He threw off the crown and shed the robe of bones.

"You're not going anywhere without me."

22

A FEW TOO MANY ZOMBIES

"What about searching for the unicorn?" asked Petunia. "We left everyone to fend for themselves back at school because you said it was the only way. We'd be lucky if any of them are still human."

"There is no unicorn," said Charles. "I was wrong. The zombie control lever was a lie. But there might be a way to stop the zombies without it. We just have to get back to Scary School."

"Even at my fastest dragon speed, that would take hours," said Dr. Dragonbreath. "Longer if we're dragging this giant along."

Drobna hung her head. "If it's true there's no unicorn, I have no hope of wishing to be taller and going back to my family. I'll just head back to my mountain."

Tears started falling from her giants eyes, drenching Johnny and Peter standing below her.

Penny stomped her foot and motioned to her. Charles interpreted for her. "Penny is saying that she wants you to come with us to Scary School. There's always a place for kids who are different there. I agree with her."

"Really?" said Drobna. "But won't I slow you down?"

"If we're slower, then we're slower," said Charles. "I'm not leaving you behind again."

Penny beamed, then ran to Charles and hugged him.

"Remarkable," said Barry.

The students jumped noticing Barry was a living creature for the first time and not a weird rock.

"Sorry, this is my friend, Barry," said Charles. "A bog monster and former monster king."

"*He* was a monster king?" said Fred. "I guess if Toothpick can be a monster king, I'll believe anything. No offense, Barry."

"Offense taken. However, now that I see the good that humans are capable of, I'm thinking maybe I was wrong about you. Perhaps you're worth saving after all. Calibus! Marcellus!"

Suddenly, two enormous white bears appeared out of thin air.

"Polter-bears!" said Charles. "Just like the ones we rode to Scream Academy."

"That's right," said Barry. "They're my bodyguards and mode of transportation. Every ex-monster king gets a pair. They are yours to borrow for the journey."

"What are polter-bears?" said Drobna.

"Poltergeist bears that can travel miles at a time through ghost portals," said Charles. "Riding them, we should be back at school in just a few minutes"

Back at Scary School, it was all terror and mayhem. And not the good kind that parents paid a lot of money for their kids to usually experience.

While Charles was searching the bog and the other students were lost in Scary Forest, the walls had been breached and dozens of zombies were pouring in by the second.

Luckily, Principal Headcrusher had ordered the school to perform an hour of zombie invasion drills every day and a plan was in place. Whether the plan had any chance of working was anybody's guess.

"Remember," Principal Headcrusher shouted to the student body that had gathered at the slayground, "the goal is to evade the zombies. You are still not allowed to kill them!"

The first wave of zombies slogged toward them, snarling and moaning, "Braaaains. Braaaains."

Each student lined up and followed the one safe path through the slayground. They had spent weeks practicing swimming across gator pond, leaping across the lava river, avoiding the quicksand box, and dodging the jungle gym's swinging axe blade.

Once every student was safely on the other side, the gators that lurked beneath scary slide lined up and formed a barrier. They snapped their gator jaws as the zombies approached.

The zombies were frightened by the gators and backed away, at first. But as more zombies poured through the walls, they pushed forward toward the reptiles.

The first zombies got clamped by the gators and tossed to the side, the next wave pounced on the gators and tried to bite them. The gator's hard scales protected them, but after a few minutes, ten zombies munching on the same spot opened a wound and one of the gators was turned into a gator zombie!

It went after the gator next to it and the rest of the gators dove back into the pond to escape.

The students were sure that the lava river would stop them in their tracks since zombies are notoriously bad jumpers. The zombies halted at the lava river and seemed to have no way across… at first.

They grunted and growled at each other, forming an idea. Then, they started doing the grossest thing anyone had ever seen. Hundreds of zombies pulled off all of their arms and started weaving them together like a basket. When it got long enough, they flung the connection of arms across the lava river, creating a suspension bridge of disgusting zombie limbs.

As the zombies crossed the bridge, the students became panic stricken. A few of the zombies fell into the quicksand box but the rest just walked on top of their heads and crossed over with ease.

The zombies that fell through the quicksand box ended up in the supply closet of Petrified Pavilion very confused.

Dozens of zombies had limbs chopped off by the axe blade, but it didn't stop them from marching forward.

"Okay," said Principal Headcrusher. "It's time for Plan B. Mrs. T, get into position!"
The T-Rex librarian stomped toward the back perimeter wall and extended her tail stiff to the ground so that it

became a ramp. Then she lifted her muzzle to the top of the wall. The students lined up from youngest to oldest and started dashing up Mrs. T. Once at the top off the wall, they jumped onto a trampoline they had set up in advance.

The zombies that would have normally been waiting for them at the bottom of the wall had followed the herd to the other side where thousands of them continued to enter the school area like a bursting dam.

"Hurry up!" shouted Fritz to the students ahead of him. "I need to get to Scary Pool where I can swim to safety!"

Steven Kingsley was hiding underneath Mrs. T busily writing down everything that was happening.

Tanya Tarantula tried shooting her leg hairs into the zombies' eyes but that didn't slow them and just made them madder.

The zombies were moments away and half the students still hadn't made it over the wall.

Principal Headcrusher looked torn. She wanted to stand in front of the zombies and protect her students, but was scared of what she might do with her massive hands if she were turned into one.

The students were panicking and started pushing the line forward up Mrs. T, causing many to lose their balance and fall off the dinosaur to the ground.

It looked like hundreds of students were doomed to have their brains eaten by zombies, but that's when one student had a terrific idea.

Marnie, the girl who was so fragile she wore a thick rubber suit to school every day to keep out germs, ran out in front of the zombies and shouted, "Hey, you creeps! Come and eat me!"

The hungry zombies pounced on her in a massive swarm, gnashing and growling, but her perfectly designed suit was so tough and air-tight, not a single zombie bite could break through it.

That gave the rest of the students the time they needed to pick themselves up and hustle up Mrs. T to the top of the wall. The last students made it out.

When the zombies finally managed to break through Marnie's suit, Chunky the doll charged through, slashing the zombies legs and faces with a shard of broken glass.

The zombies got spooked and backed away from Marnie as Chunky ran in circles shrieking "I'll murder all of you! Aaaah!" With the zombies frozen in fright, Marnie picked up Chunky and ran up Mrs. T.

"You do care about me!" said Marnie to Chunky.

"Ha!" said Chunky. "I wanna be the one to kill you, not these filthy dead guys!"

Marnie smiled at him, and he added, "Okay, maybe I care a little. So let's get out of here!"

Marnie jumped off the wall, making her the last one out.

All of the students had made it out safe.
Unfortunately, the plan had one fatal flaw.

The zombies had reached Mrs. T and were biting her legs and tail.

While the students were standing around wondering what to do next, Mrs. T was turning into a zombie T-Rex.

23

THE END OF SCARY SCHOOL

"Wow. Everyone is alive?" said Principal Headcrusher, not hiding her suprise. "And nobody got bitten?"

Rachael raised her hand, "I'm getting bit right now," she said pointing to Bryce the vampire kid, who was biting her neck.

"I meant by zombies," said Principal Headcrusher.

"I know," said Rachael, I just wanted everyone to know Bryce was biting me. Every girl had a crush on Bryce and was jealous.

Frank (which is pronounced Rachel) raised her hand.

"What is it Frank?" said Principal Headcrusher.

"I'm almost at three million jumps on my invisible jump rope! Once I pass it, it will be a world record!"

"This isn't the time for that!" said Principal Headcrusher.

"I disagree," said Lindsey. "I think we should celebrate Frank's accomplishment with a dance party. Who wants to be my date?"

Cindy Chan, who was so nervous she hardly ever spoke raised her hand, "W-w-wook over th-th-there."

Cindy pointed to the school building. The zombies had spotted them from the windows and were pouring out of the doors toward them.

"Great," said Lindsey to Cindy. "Always spoiling the party."

Suddenly there was an earthshaking roar.

"Oh no," said Principal Headcrusher. "That sounded like…"

Something massive hit the wall from the inside. Then another impact shook the ground. The wall buckled. The kids started backing away. A third impact and Mrs. T, now a zombie T-Rex, burst through, her eyes glowing red and her stomach starving for brains.

"Nobody knew where to go. The school building was flooded with zombies and the ones they had just escaped from were pouring through the gap Mrs. T had created.

The three sisters, Sarah, Lily and Mia huddled together.

Jacqueline asked them, "Can't you do your knockout spell again?"

"Sorry," said Sarah.

"That spell only works once on kids," said Lily.

"Like the chicken pox," said Mia.

Then Mia saw something over Sarah's shoulder in the distance. Petrified Pavilion was beckoning them to her with her branch hands.

"The tree is summoning us," said Mia.

"Yes, the tree," said Sarah and Lily.

The sisters signaled the other members of the P.e.p. S.q.u.a.d. and they started running toward Petrified Pavilion.

The other students were running frantically to avoid the zombie T-Rex. The Hall Monitor Mrs. Hydra jumped in between Mrs. T and the children and said, "Mrs. T, lissssten to how loud you are being. Is thisss anyway for a librarian to act?"

Mrs. T was in a frenzy and couldn't feel anything but her hunger for brains. She lunged at Ms. Hydra. Eight of Ms. Hydra's nine heads ducked out of the way, but the ninth one got bit and turned into a zombie. It started trying to bite the other nine heads, which were swerving and swinging to avoid the zombie-head, but eventually another one got bit and another and another until all nine heads were zombies and now the kids also had to deal with a zombie hydra.

Mrs. T, and Ms. Hydra started working together. They blocked off the students' escape routes from different sides while the thousands of zombies from inside the school were closing in on them from the other direction.

"They're herding us like cattle so we're easier to catch!" shouted Benny Porter the ghost.

The only way of escape was where nobody wanted to go. When she saw the P.e.p. S.q.u.a.d. making a break for Petrified Pavilion, Principal Headcrusher shouted, "Not in there! We'll be trapped inside and easier to catch!"

"Trust us!" Jacqueline shouted back as she and the sisters and Tanya Tarantula scurried toward the enormous tree.

With no other options, the students and teachers followed the P.e.p. S.q.u.a.d. to Petrified Pavilion. Usually the tree would lower its hands to feed the students into its entrance, but this time she reached out her long branches toward the ground and gathered everyone around her trunk like giving them a hug.

Principal Headcrusher said, "What are you doing? Lift us up!"

"There is no time," said Petrified Pavilion in a voice that was both feminine and deep as a pipe organ. "Too many of you would perish."

The students were frozen in shock. "You... you can talk?" said Principal Headcrusher.   "Yes. I've never been a chatter-bark like my sister Lumberella. That's why I left her and came here for some peace and quiet. My name is Treanna. The P.e.p. S.q.u.a.d. has been kind to me. When you are kind to a tree, a tree is kind back."

ZOMBIE TYRANNOSAURUS REX!

The thousands of zombies, the T-Rex, and the Hydra began closing in on them, ready to strike, but Treanna was guarding them with her branches.

"Zombies care nothing for trees," said Treanna. "I cannot allow them to turn you."

Just as the zombies and Mrs. T and Ms. Hydra surged forward to tear away the branches and bite the students, Treanna swept her arm-branches across the ground.

The enormity of her arms cleared the zombies away like sweeping sand across a floor. Even Mrs. T and Ms. Hydra tumbled across the yard.

For a moment the students could relax.

Then, a portal opened. Through it arrived the polter-bears carrying Charles, Penny, Petunia, Jason, Fred, Wendy, Lattie, Johnny, and Peter, with Dr. Dragonbreath and Drobna holding on to their tails.

"Good," said Dr. Dragonbreath. "There are survivors."

"Not for long," said Principal Headcrusher. "The pavilion saved us for now, but the zombies will keep coming, with Mrs. T and Ms. Hydra among them. Eventually they'll break through and we'll be done for."

"Ms. Hydra," said Dr. Dragonbreath. "Dear no. It can't be." Dr. Dragonbreath and Ms. Hydra had been secretly dating for several months.

Charles hopped off the polter-bear and faced the students. They all booed him.

"Okay, I deserved that," said Charles. "I thought it would be better to be the monster king, but I realized I was wrong. I belong here with my friends."

"Nobody likes you, Toothpick!" Benny Porter shouted.

"Understandable," said Charles. "All I can say is I'm sorry."

"Stop apologizing!" said Principal Headcrusher. "Did you find the unicorn or not?"

"No," said Charles. "I didn't."

"You stink, Toothpick!" Benny shouted again.

"But that's because there is no unicorn," Charles continued. "On my quest, I learned the true nature of zombies. They follow the zombies they admire. And perhaps the most admired zombie is our own extreme sports superstar."

"Ramon?" said Ramon's best friends Johnny and Peter.

"That's right," said Charles. "If we can focus on turning him back to good, the rest of the zombies may follow."

"But how do we find him in this sea of zombies?" said Petunia.

"We're his best friends," said Johnny wrapping his arm around Peter. "We can spot him anywhere."

The zombies were starting to come to after being knocked down by Treanna. They picked themselves up and were heading back toward the students.

"I just need a view into the horde," said Peter.

"I can help with that," said Treanna. She scooped Johnny and Peter into her palm and lifted them above the zombie horde.

"There he is!" Johnny pointed in a spot right in front of Mrs. T the zombie T-Rex.

"Uh oh. This might be tricky," said Treanna.

She tried to pick up Ramon, but each time she got close, Mrs. T would snap her mighty jaws and bite one of her branch fingers off.

Peter got so mad he transformed into Peter the wolf. "Get away from my friend, or I'm going to come at you like a wolf!" Peter growled.

Mrs. T wouldn't stop snapping, so Peter the wolf leaped off the branch and landed right on Mrs. T's snout. He slashed at her nose, causing her to whip her head and thrash in anguish.

That gave Treanna the opening she needed and she was able to scoop up Ramon. Peter leaped off Mrs. T's snout and landed back in Treanna's palm while Johnny kept Ramon in a headlock so he couldn't bite either of them.

"Good work, Peter!" said Johnny.

"You too!" said Peter the wolf turning back into regular Peter. Treanna dropped Ramon and his friends in the clearing in front of the students. The oncoming zombies were still approaching, but Treanna was using her other arm to shield Ramon, Johnny, and Peter. When she tried swiping the zombies again, they ducked down or dove out of the way.

"You only have a few minutes," said Treanna. "The zombies figured out how to avoid my arm-swipe. You have to turn your friend to good now or it will be all over."

Then, Mrs. T broke the through crowd of zombies, charging at full speed. She was about to take out dozens of students at once, but then Drobna the giant girl stepped in front of her and grabbed her by the throat. Drobna was bigger and stronger than the mighty T-Rex, so she could only thrash about while Drobna held onto her with all her strength.

"Hurry up!" said Drobna. "I can't hold this dinosaur for long!"

Charles approached Ramon, who still had the crazy zombie look in his eye and was desperately gnashing his teeth at Charles's deliciously egg-shaped head. Johnny and Peter did their best to hold him in place.

"Ramon, it's me. Charles Nukid. I'm your friend and so is everyone you're looking at. Isn't it time to stop this madness and go back to being the Ramon everyone liked?"

Ramon thought for a moment, then went right back to gnashing.

Petunia stepped forward. "Hey Ramon," she said. "Remember that time when you swatted the bugs around my hair and I got so mad I started crying? Ever since that happened we've been through so much together and become friends even though I didn't like you at first. Don't you want to be friends again?"

Ramon thought for a moment, then kept gnashing.

Suddenly, Ramon broke free from Johnny and Peter's grip. He made a mad dash at Charles and was a split second from biting him.

That's when I decided to do something I hadn't done since Charles Nukid's first day of school when I warned him about Dr. Dragonbreath's Rule Number Five. I decided to intervene. I made myself visible and flew between Ramon and Charles so Ramon bit me instead of him.

Never before in recorded history had a zombie actually bitten a ghost. A strange thing happened. Turns out when something that's dead bites another thing that's dead, it's like multiplying two negative numbers and it creates a positive. My ghostly form vanished and I became flesh and blood Derek once again!

"Derek? Is that you?" said Charles.

"Yeah," I said. "That's two you owe me."

Peter and Johnny quickly pulled Ramon back before he could make another lunge, or else I would have enjoyed a very short time as a living human once again.

"Time is running out," I said to Charles. "The zombies will be upon us in moments."

Charles racked his brain. "If only we knew what made Ramon so angry," he said. "But what could that be?"

Petunia thought hard and said, "Last time he was his regular self he looked like he was having a great time at the Dance of Destiny."

"The Dance of Destiny! I missed it completely," said Charles. "That's why I couldn't figure it out. What happened at the dance?"

"Everyone was dancing, but then Ramon went crazy out of nowhere. All the other zombies went bad right after Principal Headcrusher held him outside the entrance so the school's zombies saw him."

"Wait a second. Ramon was dancing? With who?"

"His date. Duhhh."

"Who was his date?"

Frank (which is pronounced Rachel) stepped forward, still furiously jumping rope. "I was his date, but don't distract me, I'm like, thirty seconds away from breaking the world record for invisible jump-roping. It's taken me eight years to get to this point."

Charles looked around. The zombies were less than ten seconds away from the students.

Lattie leaped out in front and threw all her last ninja stars and sais but there were too many zombies for them to have much affect.

The students and teachers huddled together and braced themselves for a thousand zombie bites.

"Quick," said Charles. "Do you remember the moment Ramon went crazy?"

"Sure," said Frank. "He tried to kiss me, but my invisible jump rope kept hitting him in the face. He didn't even get close."

"Did you want to kiss him?" asked Petunia.

"Oh yeah," said Frank to Petunia. "I told you how much I have a crush on him. But I couldn't stop jumping rope, could I? I'd have to start all over."

"Frank, this is the answer!" exclaimed Charles. "You have to kiss Ramon. He must have a crush on you too, so when your rope hit him in the face, it drove him crazy!"

"Really? You think he as a crush on me, too?"

"Yes! Now kiss him before we all die!"

"But I'm about to break the jump rope world record."

"We're all going to die before you break the record!"

"Ughhh… fine."

Frank put down the invisible jump rope and the invisible counter reset itself from 2,999,999 to zero.

She learned forward, avoided Ramon's snapping teeth, and kissed him on the cheek.

Ramon snapping teeth immediately became still. His bloodshot eyes went back to white and he smiled bigger than he ever had before.

"Whoo hoo!" shouted Ramon. "I got a kiss from Frank! (pronounced Rachel) Hey? Why am I down here? Isn't the Dance of Destiny up there?"

As Charles looked around he noticed that all of the zombies were coming out of a daze and were looking around, mystified.

Mrs. T the T-Rex and Ms. Hydra were back to normal.

"Oh thank goodness," said Mrs. T. "The zombie-ness hadn't fully settled in and we're back to ourselves. Mr. Acidbath, Dr. Jeckyll, and Ms. Medusa joined them, all back to themselves.

Mrs. T turned to Drobna the giant girl. "Thank you for stopping me from eating the students, deary. Nobody deserves to get eaten who doesn't make noise in the library."

All of the students gathered around Drobna and hugged her giant legs for saving their lives.

"Glad I could help," said Drobna.

Charles stepped in and explained how Drobna had run away from home and had been searching for the unicorn to grant her a wish and make her taller so she could go back home.

"What a heart-wrenching tale," said Mrs. T, "How would you like to attend Scary School on a free scholarship? I *am* in charge of admissions."

"But what about her giant family?" said Principal Headcrusher. "Shouldn't we get their permission?"

"No," said Drobna. "Those who would kick me out for being small aren't my real family. You know, in a way, my wish has already been granted. Here at Scary School, I think I've finally found a real family, because you accept me for who I am."

The goblins from Goblin Hill, no longer zombie goblins, tumbled into the scene with their out-of-tune instruments and started playing terrible music.

The zombies and all the students started dancing together. Lindsey finally got the party she wanted and had a great time dancing with Fred. And Johnny. And Fritz.

Halfway around the world, Queen Stingbottom stood on the front lines before an army of monsters about to face off against thousands of zombies that had invaded Monster Castle.

Thinking the monsters stood no chance, Turlock the tiny troll had joined the zombies and allowed himself to get bitten in hopes of becoming the zombie king.

But right before the battle could begin, the zombies all switched back to good, shook their heads in confusion, then wandered back into the wilderness.

Turlock tried to rejoin his troll friends but was sent off to go live with zombies forever.

Queen Stingbottom received a message written on a scroll via polterbear from Charles that read:

Queen Stingbottom, I hereby relinquish my crown to you. I have a feeling the other monsters will still respect you even though you never defeated me in battle. – former King Charles.

After he sent the message, Penny ran up to Charles and gave him a kiss on the cheek. Dr. Dragonbreath patted him on the back. "Perhaps human brains work better than I thought," he said. "I may allow you to keep it a bit longer, though you'd make a fine dragon one day." He turned to the group of friends who had gathered around Charles. "And let's not forget, you promised I could eat one of you for flying you to Monster Kingdom."

The eight friends gulped, wondering whom he would choose.

"Buuut, I suppose I can hold off my meal if Charles agrees to send his future children to Scary School so I have a second chance. See, I'm tough, but fair."

Charles shook Dr. Dragonbreath's claw and the friends exhaled in relief. Then Jason, Johnny, and Fred all tried to hug Petunia, but collided into one another and the fight resumed right where it had left off.

I hugged my sister, Jacqueline. Chunky popped out from the zombie horde and hugged Marnie. Wendy Crumkin hugged a bat she thought was Count Checkula. Bryce hugged Rachael. Lattie hugged Millie, her pet centipede. Dr. Dragonbreath flew over to Ms. Hydra and hugged seven of her nine heads. Two of them he didn't like very much.

Principal Headcrusher went around hugging each student and she was soon joined by all of the zombies who were so thankful to be back to their good selves. It was an all-out human-monster-zombie hug-fest.

Frank started jumping her invisible rope again. "One, two, three four... Just another three million to go," she said.

Suddenly, a portal opened and another polter-bear leaped through. On its back was Barry the bog monster.

"Hey there fellas," said Barry. "You didn't think I'd let you borrow my best multi-dimensional bear, did you?"

"You were right," said Charles to Barry. "The zombie apocalypse did start with one zombie. And deep down he was still himself. He just needed a little love to bring the good back out."

"Oh... well that's great," said Barry. "The truth is I had a change of heart and was going to give you this."

Barry pulled aside the poofy hair atop his head revealing a brilliant shimmering unicorn horn.

"Sometimes a unicorn isn't only the last place you'd expect, it's also the last *thing* you'd expect."

Then he winked at Charles and disappeared back through the portal.

The mushy moment had turned to total confusion.

"What in the world was that?" said Principal Headcrusher.

"You know what? I don't know and I don't care," said Charles. "I'm done searching for mythical beasts, wielding flaming swords, and ruling over monsters or anyone else. From now on, I just wanted to be plain old

Charles Nukid—student of Scary School, loyal friend, and follower of every rule to the letter."

"Don't forget the world's only walking toothpick!" joked Lebok the seventh-grade troll.

The students and teachers took one another's hands and started walking back toward the school building.

Hurry along, children," said Principal Headcrusher. "The end of a zombie apocalypse doesn't mean recess is any longer than normal. Next class starts in two minutes!"

The students groaned, then gathered their belongings and headed back to their classrooms.

"So," said Charles to Penny, "Would you like me to walk you to class?"
as he was told, he pulled Penny aside to their secret space between the lockers where they used to exchange candy, and he returned her kiss on the cheek.

"I don't want to miss one more dance with you. Will you be my girlfriend?" asked Charles.

"Yes," said Penny.

The force of her voice caused Charles's head to hit the side of the locker and he felt super-woozy. When he came to his senses, Penny was kissing the bump on his head. Then she handed him a piece of candy and ran off to class.

Penny said nothing, which of course meant yes.

On the way to class, Charles decided to break a rule for the first time in years. Instead of going straight to class

Charles thought to himself, if Fred is right and this is all just a dream, I hope I never wake up.

Incredible bonus illustration above courtesy of
Mr. Fischer.

BONUS CHAPTER

Dear Friends,

Because I became my human self again, I was no longer bound by my duty to write about Scary School and am once again just another student there. Benny Porter the ghost was supposed to pick up the slack, but he doesn't like writing too much, so I don't think he'll be finishing any books soon.

Anyway, it's been great spending time with you these last few years. All of your kind words, support, and funny emails gave me the fondest memories a ghost writer could possibly have. While I may not write any more about Scary School, I hope you'll enjoy my many other books that you can find at DerekTaylorKent.com.

I know I usually hide a bonus chapter for you at ScarySchool.com, but this time, I'm including it right here. I just couldn't bear the thought of you not reading this...

29 Years Later

Charles Nukid and Penny Nukid stood outside the front entrance of Scary School just as they had each morning thirty years earlier.

Between them was an eight-year-old boy with large possum eyes and a helmet of perfectly shaped hair. He was shaking with nerves.

Charles kneeled down to him. "What's wrong, Son? Aren't you excited for your first day at Scary School?"

"I thought I would be, Dad. But I'm scared."

"What could you possibly be afraid of?"

"Well, what if Archie the giant squid tries to eat me? What if Ms. Fang tries to bite me? What if Dr. Dragonbreath tries to turn me into a dragon? What if Principal Crumkin doesn't like me? What if—

"Reginald Stingbottom Headcrusher Nukid, those are very good things to be afraid of. But if Ms. Fang bites you, I'm sure Nurse Hairymoles will give you someone else's blood. If Dr. Dragonbreath makes you a dragon, you would be the coolest kid in school. If Principal Crumkin doesn't like you, ask her to play a game of checkers. And if Archie tries to eat you, well, the trick is to always have a fresh crab on hand. He prefers them to children."

Reginald smiled, feeling much more relaxed.

Penny kneeled down, gave him a big hug, then gazed at his face, forcing herself to remember every detail of her son's features in case he came back missing a nose or an appendage.

Reginald turned and started to walk across the drawbridge.

"Wait!" said Charles. "If you don't want to turn into a dragon, never read Rule Number Five."

Charles had sworn to himself he wouldn't let his son know that in advance and deny Dr. Dragonbreath yet another opportunity for a Nukid dragon, but at that moment he figured, like father like son.

"Thanks, Dad," said Reginald.

Charles wiped away a tear in his eye as his son turned and walked away.

Standing at the drawbridge, Reginald was joined by a purple girl who looked just as scared as he did. They held hands and ran across the bridge together, sliding beneath Archie's tentacles and making it into the locker hallway safely.

Once he was out of sight, Charles and Penny hugged for what felt like an eternity. Neither wanted to let the other go.

The whole time Charles was thinking to himself, I definitely made the right decision.

THE END

NOW I LIKE BATHS!

DEREK THE GHOST

AKA Derek Taylor Kent

is the author of the *Scary School* series as well as the picture books *El Perro Con Sombrero* and *Simon and the Solar System.* Other middle grade books include *Rudy and the Beast: My Homework Ate My Dog!* and *Principal Mikey.* You can visit him at DerekTaylorKent.com for more information on all his books and other projects. You can also have a whole lot of fun reading secret chapters, playing games, and touring the Scary School at ScarySchool.com.

REVO YANSON

is a visual artist/painter, illustrator and animator. He earned his fine arts degree at La Consolacion College of Arts. He co-founded KAMI art group and Rhymes of Resistance – a monthly poetry reading session in Bacolod, Philippines. At present, he serves as the chairman of DIHON Art Collective. He is currently the editorial cartoonist of Sunstar Newspaper. His works can be seen at www.byrevo.com and www. Revoyanson.com.